PRAISE FO
& RIC

"A pleasure . . . Westlake's ability to construct
an action story filled with unforeseen twists
and quadruple-crosses is unparalleled."
San Francisco Chronicle

"The best Grofield star vehicle yet."
NICK JONES, *Existential Ennui* (blog)

"Plenty of action . . . Grofield demonstrates his
expertise in putting down a dangerous conspiracy."
Best Sellers

"Never before has Grofield gone for so many
rides with someone else at the wheel."
New York Times

"Energy and imagination light up virtually
every page, as does some of the best hard-
boiled prose ever to grace the noir genre."
Publishers Weekly

"Grofield succeeds in all he needs to do with
endurance, incongruity and a lot of valid humour."
Times Literary Supplement

The Blackbird

GROFIELD NOVELS BY RICHARD STARK

The Damsel
The Dame
The Blackbird
The Sour Lemon Score

PARKER NOVELS BY RICHARD STARK

The Hunter (Payback)
The Man with the Getaway Face
The Outfit
The Mourner
The Score
The Jugger
The Seventh
The Handle
The Rare Coin Score
The Green Eagle Score
The Black Ice Score
The Sour Lemon Score
Deadly Edge
Slayground
Plunder Squad
Butcher's Moon
Comeback
Backflash
Flashfire
Firebreak
Breakout
Nobody Runs Forever
Ask the Parrot
Dirty Money

Information about the complete list of Richard Stark books published by the University of Chicago Press—and electronic editions of them—can be found on our website: http://www.press.uchicago.edu/.

The Blackbird

An Alan Grofield Novel

Richard Stark

WITH A NEW FOREWORD
BY SARAH WEINMAN

The University of Chicago Press

The University of Chicago Press, Chicago, 60637
University of Chicago Press edition 2012
Printed in the United States of America

21 20 19 18 17 16 15 14 13 12   1 2 3 4 5

ISBN-13: 978-0-226-77042-0 (paper)
ISBN-10: 0-226-77042-7 (paper)

Library of Congress Cataloging-in-Publication Data

Stark, Richard, 1933–2008.
  The blackbird : an Alan Grofield novel / Richard Stark ; with a new
foreword by Sarah Weinman.
      p. cm.
    ISBN-13: 978-0-226-77042-0 (paperback : alkaline paper)
    ISBN-10: 0-226-77042-7 (paperback : alkaline paper)
    I. Title.
    PS3573.E9B565 2012
    813'.54—DC23

                              2011032945

♾ This paper meets the requirements of ANSI/
NISO Z39.48-1992 (Permanence of Paper).

FOREWORD

IF YOU ARE BRAND NEW to the works of Richard Stark, my advice would be to put down this book for a while and acquaint yourself first with the many other noir crime novels featuring Stark's main man Parker, that merciless and iconic antihero. Once you're finished working your way through those small masterpieces, you'll be ready to tackle these three entertaining tales (as well as a fourth) starring Parker's quick-witted, dapper companion in heisting, Alan Grofield.

Grofield, who first appeared in *The Score* (1964), isn't exactly Watson to Parker's Holmes—the very idea is discombobulating—but like Conan Doyle's go-to narrator, Grofield himself leads a double professional life. "I'm an actor," he explains in *The Damsel* (1967), "and it's impossible to make ends meet these days as an actor in the legitimate theater. Unless you're willing to peddle your integrity to the movie and television people, there's nothing to it.... Do you realize that in my peak year so far I earned a measly thirty-seven hundred dollars from acting?"

For Alan Grofield, you see, has principles, at least applied to artistic pursuits. No movies or television. His greatest love is the theater, and he channels this love by way of summer stock, operating a small troupe in the Midwest. Is it a living? Hardly. Which is why he turns to more illicit means of funding his theatrical enterprises. Early on in *The Dame* (1969), Grofield describes his origin story in criminal enterprise: he started off nervous his first time, since this whole heist business seemed so alien to his day-to-day life. But two jobs later, he'd graduated from amateur to pro, and by the time we meet him in *The Score*, Grofield is well-seasoned to the point where a hard man like Parker, wary and distrustful in the best of times, doesn't think twice about turning to him for the tightest of tight spots.

Alan Grofield appeared in print a grand total of eight times—four times as Parker's adjunct, and four times on his own. As a sidekick, Grofield's bon vivant nature emerged in snippets, but he never overshadowed Parker. If anything, Stark seemed to underplay Grofield such that he lit up the page almost by accident—his wit, skirt chasing, and Shakespeare quotes offering a welcome break from Parker's tough, stoic worldview. On his own, however, Grofield is both more present and more enigmatic, almost as if Westlake viewed him as a perpetual experiment.

Grofield was a lab rat for Westlake, who liked to experiment with tone—veering, somewhat wildly, between dark violence, witty banter, and absurdist humor—and plot. (Westlake commented that *Lemons Never Lie* [1971] was a way for him to experiment with a narrative arc featuring multiple bounces moving higher and higher, instead of the more common parabolic plot curve.) At the same time, the Grofield novels provide a transition between the hard-edged Parker series and the more avuncular, humor-laden books Westlake published under his own name.

⁕ ⁕ ⁕

The Damsel opens when a girl climbs in Grofield's fifth-floor hotel window. He's in Mexico, coming back from the near-dead after events described in *The Handle* (a Parker novel from 1966), with a bag of money he hasn't, on account of his infirm status, gotten around to spending. His first spoken line in *The Damsel* is typical of Grofield's wit and weakness for women:"If you're my fairy godmother, I want my back scratched." After pages of witty banter, Grofield will see his itch relieved, and much more, from young Main Line lass Elly Fitzgerald. What emerges is a mix of romantic comedy and adventure that echoed Westlake's earliest ventures into humorous crime novels like *The Fugitive Pigeon* (1965) and *The Spy in the Ointment* (1966), published just a year before the first Grofield novel.

In *The Damsel*, Westlake takes some time out from traveling Mexican highways filled with action-centered plotting to enjoy a little social satire. Here the author, under the cover of Grofield's critical eye, astutely zeroes in on the community class system of the charming Mexican city San Miguel de Allende, comparing it to Greenwich Village, of all places:

> Along Macdougal and Eighth Streets the same faces could be found in all the tourist traps: the tourists themselves, looking embarrassed and irritable, and the unwashed, shaven youngsters living around here while going through their artistic phase, looking both older and younger than their years. Both the tourists and the youngsters were self-conscious, and neither could cover it all the way.
>
> But here there was a third kind of person, too. Around San Miguel there was a colony of retired people from the State, living on pensions. A thousand dollars a year was damn good money on the local economy, so these retired people could live in a climate as good as Florida or California, but at a fraction of the price. Their presence somehow made both the tourists and the youngsters look even more foolish than usual, as though somehow or other they'd been exposed as frauds. (58)

Greenwich Village was a location Westlake knew well; he lived there for decades, keeping an apartment in the neighborhood even after he moved upstate. But comparing such seemingly disparate places allows the author to zero in on specific types, see through their chosen facades for the ridiculousness underneath and show how human behavior remains static, even common, no matter where one is. This section is a classic example of Westlake's economy with sentences; so little says so much about so many people.

Observation and travelogue take twin top billing in *The Dame*, perhaps because Westlake doesn't seem to be all that interested in the plot, a cross between a locked-room mystery and a strung-out caper. From the very first, Grofield wonders what exactly he's doing there. The book opens with "Grofield, not knowing what it was all about"; a little later he thinks, "here he was in the middle of somebody else's story. To take a simile from his second profession, he had been miscast" (38). It should come as no surprise that one character cries out accusingly at Grofield, "God damn it, all you want to do is die a smart-ass!" (177). The net result is that, despite acts of bravery and saving people's lives, Grofield's character flaws seem unduly magnified, albeit in the way that makes the reader stay for the wild ride until the end.

Even Grofield's afterthought of a love interest can't escape from comic flourish on the part of the author, thanks to her very name, Pat Chelm: her surname is a pejorative term amongst Jews, used to denote the most foolish of a town full of fools, whose antics are so steeped in stupidity that to mock them is to do them a service. What kind of private joke Stark was engaging here is anyone's guess, but one possible clue lies in how oddly, and badly, women are treated in the Grofield novels. One must make allowances for prefeminist attitudes, but Grofield's cavalier and sometimes contempt-laden relationships with women strike a more off-key note than, say, Parker's. Parker is cruel to everyone, regardless of gender; he can objectify a CEO or a mob boss as easily as a dame. Grofield's attitude towards women is somehow less palatable. In *The Dame*, for example, he ridicules Pat Chelm while she's making a painful confession:

> "I had an abortion. I was seventeen."
> She meant Look-how-young-I-was, but Grofield didn't take it that way. "You're twenty-two now, aren't you?" he said.
> "Yes."
> "Isn't it time you got over it?" (122)

The lackadaisical loopiness of *The Dame* gives way to something a little harsher in *The Blackbird*. Its opening chapter is more or less the same as the Parker masterpiece *Slayground* (the scheduling quirks of publishing meant that even though the books may have been written roughly around the same time, *The Blackbird* was published in 1969, two years before *Slayground*). But here Stark follows Grofield's path up north to Quebec City's sumptuous Chateau Frontenac Hotel and a province jittery with dissident behavior. Stark didn't spell it out—the setting, despite political overtones, seems more rooted in past vacationing by the author—but the province, and eventually the country, would be gripped by the actions of a breakaway group called the FLQ that advocated, violently, for Quebec's separation from the rest of the English-speaking country.

He is, however, fairly resourceful in *The Blackbird*. Finding himself locked in a basement, Grofield escapes through common sense and some degree of ingenuity, as Stark describes in typically matter-of-fact fashion, with the help of available tools and a good sense of spatial memory. He also digs deep to find his inner Parker, a surprising turn made more so, because Grofield spent the past two and a half books not taking himself terribly seriously—and as a result, the reader, lulled into relaxation, is shocked out of it.

Grofield's recaptured killer instinct serves him well in *Lemons Never Lie* (1971), which brings him back to his original, Parker-level noir roots. Further experiments in comedic tone and literary playfulness emerged thereafter under the Westlake name—for example, one of the Dortmunder novels, *Jimmy the Kid*, even patterned its plot after a fictional Parker novel. Ironically, in introducing Dortmunder, Westlake pulled one last rabbit out of his hat with respect to Grofield, using his name as the alter for one of Dortmunder's cronies in crime, the "charming ladies' man" Alan Greenwood. (Trent Reynolds, who maintains the Violent World of Parker fan website, looks on Greenwood's appropriation of "Grofield" as a parody of the original. I'm not sure I'd go that far, but it's another nice touch of self-reference from a writer who clearly enjoyed it.)

Grofield would appear only one more time, in *Butcher's Moon*, which seemed to put the Stark pseudonym on ice for good. Grofield had served his purpose as a means of distinguishing between Westlake and Stark; it was as if the actor, having adopted so many different guises in playing both theatrical and criminal roles, represented Westlake's own experiments with multiple styles. Consider, too, that after 1974, Westlake used fewer pseudonyms—just Samuel Holt in the 1980s and Judson Jack Carmichael in the 1990s—than earlier in his career, when Westlake published as Tucker Coe, Alan Marsh, and Curt Clark, among many other names. Dortmunder provided the final break between the comedic Westlake and the noirish Stark, but Grofield, unwittingly, helped force the Stark pseudonym underground for more than twenty years until his (and Parker's) triumphant return in the late 1990s, never to leave until Westlake himself shuffled off of this mortal coil.

Sarah Weinman

The Blackbird

ONE

GROFIELD JUMPED OUT of the Ford with a gun in one hand and the empty satchel in the other. Parker was out and running too, and Laufman stayed hunched over the wheel, his foot tapping the accelerator.

The armored car lay on its side in a snowbank, its wheels turning like a dog chasing rabbits in its sleep. The mine had hit it just right, flipping it over without blowing it apart. There was a sharp metallic smell all around, and the echo of the explosion seemed to twang in the cold air, richocheting from the telephone wires up above. Cold winter afternoon sunlight made all the shadows sharp and black.

Grofield ran to the front of the armored car, running around the big old-fashioned grill, sideways now at chest level. Through the bulletproof windshield he could see the uniformed driver in there, turned every which way but conscious and moving around, getting a phone receiver out from under the dashboard.

The day was cold, but Grofield's face was sleek with perspiration. He raised a hand to his mouth and was surprised when he touched cloth, forgetting for just a second the mask he was wear-ing. The hand he'd raised was the one with the gun in it, and that surprised him too. He felt disoriented, weightless, invisible, an actor who's walked through a door onto the wrong set.

In a way that was true. He *was* an actor, a legitimate stage actor, at some times, but that was no way to earn a living. He earned it this way, with a gun in his hand and a mask on his face.

So it was time to get back into the right part. After the smallest of hesitations he moved forward again, heading for the driver's compartment. Inside there, the driver was talking quickly into his phone, watching Grofield with nervous eyes.

Both doors were intact. The explosion should have sprung at least one of them, but it hadn't. There was no way to get in at the driver.

Grofield heard the second explosion, short and flat and unim-pressive, and the armored car jerked like a wounded horse. That would have been Parker, blowing the back door.

Grofield gave up on the driver and hurried to the rear of the armored car, where the door was now hanging open at a weird angle. There was nothing but blackness inside.

Grofield said, "He's on his phone in there and I can't get at him."

Parker nodded. There were no sirens yet. They were in the middle of a large city, but it was the most isolated spot on this armored car's route, a straight and little-traveled road across mostly undeveloped flats from one built-up section to another. At this point the road was flanked by high wooden fences set back on both sides, the gray fence on the left being around the ball-park and the green one on the right being around an amusement park. Both of them were closed at this time of year, and there were no private homes or open businesses within sight.

Parker rapped his gun against the metal of the armored car. "Come out easy," he called. "We don't want anybody dead, all we want is money." When there was no response he called, "Make us do it the hard way, we'll drop a grenade in there with you."

A voice called from inside, "My partner's unconscious."

"Drag him out here."

There was a shuffling sound from inside, as though they'd uncovered a mouse nest. Grofield waited awkwardly, his role calling for nothing from him right now. Movement he could handle, but waiting and wounded people were problems. They didn't exist onstage.

The blue-coated guard backed out, finally, bent over, pulling his partner by the armpits. The partner had a bloody nose.

As soon as they were out, Grofield handed the empty satchel to Parker, who ducked and went inside. Grofield showed the gun in his hand to the conscious guard, who looked at it with sullenness and respect.

The other one was lying on his back in the snow, dark red blood trickling across his cheeks, and the conscious one stood over him with worried looks, not knowing what to do about him. Grofield said, "Put some snow on the back of his neck. You want to make sure he doesn't strangle on his blood."

The guard nodded. He went to his knees beside the unconscious man, rolled him onto his side, held a handful of snow to the back of his neck.

A siren, far away. Grofield and the guard both raised their heads, like deer scenting a hunter. Grofield glanced back at the Ford, and Laufman was staring this way, his face round and nervous. Exhaust was coming out of the Ford in white puffs like smoke signals, because Laufman's foot was jittering on the accelerator.

Grofield looked back at the guard, who was still kneeling there pressing snow to the other man's neck. Their eyes met, and then Parker came back out of the armored car, carrying the satchel, now obviously full. The siren was still far away, it didn't seem to get any closer, but that didn't mean anything.

Parker nodded to Grofield, and the two of them ran back to the Ford. They clambered in, Grofield in front next to Laufman, Parker in back with the satchel, and Laufman stood on the accelerator. Wheels spun on ice and the Ford slued its rear end leftward. Grofield braced his hands against the dashboard, grimacing with strain.

"Easy!" Parker shouted from the back seat. "Take it easy, Laufman!"

Laufman finally eased off on the accelerator enough so the wheels could grab, and then they started moving, the Ford lunging down the road. It was like hurrying down the middle of a snowy football field with a high gray fence on the left sideline and a high green fence on the right and the goalposts way the hell around the curve of the Earth somewhere.

Far away ahead of them they saw the dot of flashing red light. Laufman yelled, "I'll have to take the other route!" Grofield, glancing over at him, saw Laufman's face white and wide-eyed with panic. His fists seemed welded to the steering wheel.

"Do it, then!" Parker told him. "Don't talk about it."

They'd worked out three ways to leave here, depending on circumstances. The one behind them they'd ignored, the one ahead was no good any more. For the third one, they should take the right at the end of the green fence, go almost all the way around the amusement park and wind up in a neighborhood of tenements and vacant lots where they had three potential places laid out to ditch the Ford.

They had plenty of time. The end of the fence was just ahead, and the flashing red light was still a mile or more away. But Laufman was still standing on the accelerator. They had known Laufman was a second-rate driver, but he was the best they could find for this job and he did know the city. But he was coming too fast at the intersection, way too fast.

Grofield was still braced against the dashboard, panic flickering now in the back of his mind. "Laufman!" he shouted. "Slow down! You won't make the turn!"

"I know how to drive!" Laufman screamed, and spun the wheel without any deceleration at all. The side road shot by on an angle, the car bucked, it dug its left shoulder into the pavement and started to roll.

Grofield's hands could no longer push the dashboard away. The world outside the windshield was going topsy-turvy, flashes of white ground and white sky, a gray chain-link fence rushing closer, the windshield rushing closer, and Grofield opened his mouth to say *no* but all the white turned black before he had a chance to say it.

TWO

". . . when he wakes up."

"He is awake," Grofield said, and was so surprised to hear himself speak he opened his eyes.

Hospital. Himself in bed. Two thin thirtyish men in dark business suits standing at the foot of the bed, their heads turning to look at him. "Well, well," one of them said. "The sleeper wakes."

"Have you been listening?" the other one asked. "Or do we have to fill you in?"

Grofield had been filling himself in, remembering the holdup, the getaway, Laufman going into panic, the car rolling over and over, and then the abrupt lights out. And now? He was in a hospital, those two guys weren't doctors, the future didn't look bright. He looked at them standing there and said, "You're cops."

"Not exactly," the second one said. He came around the foot of the bed and sat down in the chair to Grofield's left. At the same time, the first one moved farther away, over to the door, and stood there casually, arms folded, back against the door.

Grofield found it painful to turn his head and dizzying to look at the seated one through his nose, so he shut the off eye and said, "Nobody's not exactly a cop. Not exactly means not local."

The seated one smiled. "Very good, Mr. Grofield," he said.

Grofield squinted the open eye. "You have my name."

"We have you cold, my friend. Name, prints, history, everything. You've been a lucky boy up till now."

"That was the first time I was ever involved in anything like that," Grofield lied.

The other's smile turned sardonic. "Not likely," he said. "Laufman is a pro. The one who got away is a pro. They brought in an amateur to help out? Not likely.

So Parker had gotten away. Grofield said, "With or without the money?"

"What?"

"Somebody got away. With or without the money?"

The one at the door barked, but when Grofield looked at him in astonishment he saw the bark had been intended as a laugh. The barker said, "He'd like to go collect his share."

"A workman wants his wages," Grofield said. "I don't suppose there's any point my claiming I was kidnapped by those two and forced to help them."

"Oh, go ahead," said the seated one. "But not with us, we don't particularly care about the robbery."

Painful or not, Grofield turned his head and put two eyes to work studying the guy seated there. He said, "Insurance dicks?"

The barker barked again, and the seated one said, "We work for your government, Mr. Grofield. You can think of us as civil servants."

"FBI."

"Hardly."

"Why hardly? What else is there besides the FBI?"

"Your government has many arms," the seated one said, "each devoted to aid and protect you in its own way."

The room door opened, bumping the barker, who looked annoyed. A cop came in, burly and middle-aged, in uniform, with a hatbrim full of fruit salad. An important cop, an inspector or some such. He didn't quite salute, but stood poised and hesitant in the doorway, like a waiter anticipating a large tip. "Just wondering how you gentlemen are coming along," he said, smiling with curiosity and eagerness to please.

"We're doing fine," said the barker. "We'll be out in just a few minutes."

"Take your time, take your time." The cop glanced at Grofield in the bed, and for just a second his expression went kaleidoscopic, as though he didn't know what his attitude toward Grofield was supposed to be. It was impossible to read anything in the gyrations of his face except possibly that he had gone temporarily insane.

"Thank you for your interest, Captain," the seated one said, without smiling. It was a clear-cut dismissal, and the cop understood it. He began nodding and nodding, his waiter's smile flashing on and off as he said, "Well then, I'll . . ." Still nodding, not finishing the sentence, he backed out and shut the door.

The seated one said, "Is there any way to lock that?"

The barker studied the knob. "Not from this side. But I doubt he'll be back."

"We'll make it fast," the seated one said, and looked back at Grofield. He said, "I want straight answers to a couple of questions. Don't worry about self-incrimination, this is between you and us."

"Go ahead and ask," Grofield said. "I can always say no."

"Tell me what you know about General Luis Pozos."

Grofield looked at him in surprise. "Pozos? What's he got to do with anything?"

"We told you our interest wasn't the robbery. Tell me about Pozos."

"He's president of some country in Latin America. Guerrero."

"Do you know him personally?"

"In a way."

"What way?"

"I saved his life one time. Not on purpose."

"You've been a guest on his yacht?"

Grofield nodded, which was also painful. His skull seemed to have been removed and replaced with sandpaper, so that he was all right when he lay still but moving made things scrape. So he stopped nodding and said, "That was after I saved his life. Some people were going to kill him, and I ran into a girl who knew about it, and we went and broke it up."

"You aren't in contact with him now?"

Grofield restrained himself from shaking his head. "No," he said. "We don't travel in the same circles."

"Have you ever been employed by him?"

"No."

"What is your feeling about him?"

"I don't have one."

"You must have *some* feeling."

"I wouldn't want him to marry my sister."

The barker barked. The seated one smiled and said, "All right. what about a man named Onum Marba?"

"Can he marry my sister, is that what you want?"

"I want to know what you know about him."

"He's a politician from Africa. I forget the name of his country."

"Undurwa," the seated one said, with the accent on the middle syllable.

"Right. Makes me think of underwear."

The seated one made an impatient face. "Does it," he said. "Tell me about Marba."

"I never saved his life. He and I were houseguests together at a place in Puerto Rico last year, that's all."

"You never worked for him."

"No. And I'm not in contact with him now."

"And your feeling about him?"

"He's a sharp cookie. He could marry my sister."

The seated one nodded and sat back and looked at the barker. "What do you think?"

The barker studied Grofield, who met his eye and took the

brief time out to try to figure out what the heck was going on. He was a professional thief—as a means of supporting himself in the unrewarding vocation of professional actor, self-limited to the legitimate stage—and after twelve years of quiet success at his two crafts disaster had befallen. He'd appeared in a turkey, the show had folded on the road, but it looked like it would be a long, long time before he would again be, in the actor's phrase, at liberty.

But what had General Pozos from Latin America and Onum Marba from Africa to do with a busted armored car heist in a northern American city? And what had these government employees who were not with the FBI and who didn't care about the robbery to do with Alan Grofield?

The barker finished his inspection of Grofield before Grofield finished his inspection of the situation. He looked away from Grofield and nodded, saying, "Try him."

"Right." The seated one faced Grofield again. He said, "We're going to offer you a deal, and you can take it or leave it, but you'll have to decide right now."

"A deal? I'll take it."

The seated one said, "Listen to it first."

"Does it involve me going to jail?"

"Just listen," the seated one said. "We can arrange to change your status in the robbery from participant to witness. You'll sign a statement, and that will be the end of it."

Grofield said, "I'm trying to think what I have that I want badly enough to keep so you'll trade all that for it, and I don't come up with anything."

The barker said, "How's about your life?"

Grofield looked at him without moving his head. "You want me to kill myself? No deal."

It was the seated one who answered, saying, "What we want you to do will maybe risk your life. We can't know ahead of time."

Grofield looked at the two faces, then at the door the captain of police had come so obsequiously through just a minute ago, and said, "I'm getting a glimmering. It's secret agent time, espionage, all that Technicolor jazz. You birds are CIA."

The seated one made a pouting face, and the barker said, "Sometimes I can't stand it. CIA, CIA, CIA. Don't people realize their government has some *secret* intelligence organizations?"

The seated one told him, "I had an uncle in the Treasury. People had him down for an FBI man so damn much he took an early retirement."

Grofield said, "I didn't mean to offend you."

"That's all right," the seated one said. "The general public likes things clear-cut, that's all, just a few simple organizations. Like remember how happy everybody was when the Cosa Nostra first came out?"

"Like chlorophyll," the barker said. "The public loves brand names."

"And you people," Grofield said, "are brand X, is that it?"

"A perfect description," the seated one said cheerfully. "We're brand X, that's it to the life." He turned to the barker, saying, "Huh, Charlie? Is that nice?"

"Our friend has a way with words," the barker said.

The seated one smiled at Grofield, pleased with him, then grew serious again. "All right," he said. "The point is, brand X wants you to work for them. It may be dangerous, it may not, we don't know. If you agree, and if you do the job, this little jam you're in now is over and forgotten. If you refuse, or if you agree and then try to run out on us, we'll drop you back into the frying pan."

"In other words, you're offering me the fire."

"Maybe. We don't know for sure."

"What are the details?"

The seated one shook his head, smiling sadly. "Sorry. You can't open this package till after you accept delivery."

"Because," Grofield said unhappily, "if I refuse, you don't want me to know too much. Is that it?"

"Right on the money."

"And how long do I have to make up my mind?"

"Take a full minute, if you want."

"You're a sport," Grofield said. "What about Laufman, does he get the same deal?"

"No. Just you."

"He might make unhappy noises at his trial, if I'm not there."

"He isn't expected to live." At Grofield's look, he went on, "His doing, not ours. He punctured a lung, among other things."

The barker—Charlie—said, "Better make up your mind, Grofield, I hear our friends getting impatient in the hall."

"You didn't ask me if I was a patriot," Grofield reminded him.

The seated one said, "It didn't seem a relevant question. Yes or no?"

"You know it's yes, damn it. If you didn't know it, you wouldn't have asked."

The seated one smiled and stood. "We'll see you when the doctors say you're healthy," he said. "Do they call you Al or Alan?"

"Alan."

"I'm Ken, that's Charlie. See you soon."

"The minutes will seem like hours," Grofield said.

They were moving toward the door, but Ken turned back to say, "There is a certain amount of urgency involved. If you aren't ready to go in time for us to use you, naturally the deal is off." He smiled cheerily. "Get well soon," he said.

THREE

GROFIELD WALKED OUT OF the hospital into a snowstorm and the arms of Charlie and Ken. Ken said brightly, "Give you a lift?"

"No, thanks," Grofield said. "I thought I'd take the bus."

"Our car is over here," Ken said. Their hands were gently closed around Grofield's upper arms.

"You're too good to me," Grofield said, and walked with them to an unmarked Chevrolet. Not that it had to be marked; no private citizen has owned a black Chevrolet since 1939. All three got into the back seat, Grofield in the middle, and the chunky, spectacled man in the fur hat behind the wheel started them out of the parking lot.

It had been three days since Grofield's conversation with these two, plenty of time for him to get over the sense of unreality they brought with them. Counterspy stuff didn't really exist, it was invented for the convenience of novelists and screenwriters, like Atlantis and the timeless West and hippies. But Grofield had understood quickly enough that he had to start thinking of these guys and their world as real because they were likely to have some very real offects on his life, one way or another. So there *are* secret agents on the planet Earth, and two of them had invited Grofield to play on their team, and it was a game whose rules probably didn't entirely coincide with the fictional version he knew in the movies and on television. They had gotten him out of the frying pan, as promised, and now it was up to him to get himself out of the fire.

As the car entered the slow-moving, snow-clogged stream of traffic, Grofield said, "Do I get to open the package now?"

"That's what we're here for," Ken said. "The other day you invited us to ask if you were patriotic. We declined, but now I'll ask you something similar. How political are you?"

"I agree with that famous man, Whatzisname, who said, 'My country; may I never have to think about her.'"

Charlie, on Grofield's other side, barked and said, "I'm afraid you're one of the great unwashed, Alan."

"You betcha."

Ken said, "Are you political enough to know the phrase Third World?"

"Are we back to the Cosa Nostra?"

"Not exactly," Ken said. Outside, the snow was so bad you could barely see the storefronts they were passing. Ken said, "The Third World is the all-purpose journalists' term for all those nations neither in our sphere of influence nor in the Communist sphere of influence. Much of Africa, some of Latin America, a little of Asia. The filler at the United Nations."

"Poor countries, most of them," Charlie said. "Unimportant, generally."

"I suppose you don't know this," Ken said, "since most people don't, but a few years ago there was a meeting in California of one hundred of the Western world's finest brains, gathered together to discuss the probable future, and their conclusion was that the key to the future lay in the Third World. They believed that the nations of the Third World would tend more and more to military dictatorships, rule by colonel and general, and that these military men would have more in common with one another than with any of their own people or anyone at all from the United States or Russia. They suggested that these military rulers would tend more and more frequently to make short-term alliances with one another against both the Western and Eastern blocs, forcing *us* to become ever more militarily oriented, until within a century there would be no nonmilitary government left anywhere on Earth.

"A charming prospect," Grofield said.

"The prophecy," Ken said, "or warning, whatever you want to call it, didn't get much play in the press. It's easy to tell people they have to worry about a big country like the Soviet Union, or Red China, but it's tough to get the general public to take seriously the threat of Guatemala, say, or Syria, or the Congo."

"What it adds up to," Charlie said, "we're putting in burglar alarms when our real problem is termites."

"I've got the idea," Grofield said.

Ken said, "Good. What do you think of it?"

"What do I think of it?"

"Do you agree with the conclusion?"

"How the hell do I know?"

"Does it sound reasonable?"

Grofield shrugged. "Sure it sounds reasonable," he said. "What do I know about it? You can tell me anything you want, it'll sound reasonable."

"I would prefer," Ken said, "that you had some true comprehension of the problem, but we can get along without. I'll move on."

"I'm taking your word for it," Grofield told him. "I'm not a dummy, but this isn't my field, okay?"

"Okay," Ken said. "I'll move on."

"Fine. You move on."

Ken looked at him. "Did I hurt your feelings?"

"A little," Grofield said. "You know, I could take you into *my* profession and razzle-dazzle you with expertise, anybody can pull that sort of stunt."

"Which profession?"

"Either one."

"I did some acting in college."

"I'm sure you were adequate," Grofield told him.

Charlie barked, and Ken said, "I think I was just insulted. I'll move on."

"I wish you'd move on," Grofield said.

Ken said, "Have you ever been in Quebec?"

"City or province?"

"City."

"Yes."

"Do you know the Chateau Frontenac?"

"The big hotel there. Sure."

"Your friend General Pozos will be there this weekend," Ken said. "Under an assumed name."

"Pozos? I didn't think he ever got off his yacht."

"He will this weekend. Your other friend Onum Marba will also be there this weekend, also under an assumed name, part of the entourage of Colonel Rahgos, President of Undurwa. Everyone is incognito."

"I know Pozos and Marba know each other."

"The Third World rulers are more and more getting to know one another," Ken said. "Our information is probably incomplete, but so far as we now know the leaders of at least seven minor unaffiliated nations will all be at the Chateau Frontenac this weekend, incognito. Three African nations, one Central American, two South American and one Asian. There may be others."

"What's the meeting about?"

Charlie barked. "Wouldn't we like to know," he said.

"Oh," Grofield said.

"Our interest is so intense," Ken said, "that we're willing to help an armed robber beat the rap he so richly deserves, if he will help us find out."

"Why me?"

"Because you know two of those men. Because they both know you to be an adventurer, a man for hire. Will they have some use for an American like you? We hope so. We hope you can convince them."

"What if I can't?"

"A lot will depend," Ken said, "on how hard we think you've tried." He leaned forward, peering past the driver. "I think we're here," he said.

Grofield looked out at the snowstorm, and could vaguely see that they were going past iron gates. A gray stone building was just ahead. Watching it move closer he said, "Why don't you use some of your own people?"

"None of them have your qualifications," Ken said. "Wait till we're indoors, we'll have more to talk about."

"I'm sure we will," Grofield said.

The car had turned slowly around the corner of the building, and now pulled to a stop next to a black side door. Charlie pushed open the car door and climbed out into the falling snow, with Grofield behind him and Ken bringing up the rear. Charlie opened the black door and went in. Grofield, following, glanced back and saw the car in motion again, going away.

They entered a small and very hot foyer. They stood stamping off snow and opening their overcoats, and then went through another set of doors and down a narrow brown corridor to a broad maroon corridor, which they took to the left. They entered a smallish room ringed with bookcases and dominated by an oak conference table with captain's chairs. Ken said, "Sit down. We'll finish in here." There were some things at one place—folders, papers, a small metal box—and Ken sat down there.

Grofield draped his overcoat over one chair and sat in another. Ken was to his left, and Charlie took the seat opposite. Ken opened a folder and said, "I'll tell you now what we've set up for you. We have you booked in at the Chateau Frontenac for four days from Thursday, tomorrow, under your own name. We have an airline ticket for this evening, assuming any planes are taking off today, with a change at New York. A four-hour layover there, I'm sorry to say. It was the best we could do."

"Don't worry your head."

"Thank you. In addition to the clothing we gave you at the hospital, which looks very good on you by the way . . ."

"Thank you. A little conservative for my taste, but not bad."

Ken smiled thinly. "Yes. In addition to that, we have one suitcase for you with everything you should require during your stay in Quebec, changes of clothing, a razor, toothbrush, things like that."

"No miniature cameras, tape recorders, dart guns?"

Another thin smile. "Afraid not. We've also been authorized to give you some spending money. Not much by your standards, perhaps, but enough for coffee and cigarettes. One hundred dollars."

"In cash or stamps?"

The thin smile again. "It's taxpayers' money," Ken said.

Charlie said, "If they won't give their schoolteachers a living wage, you can't expect them to be lavish with amateur spies."

Grofield nodded. "I wonder what Castro would pay for the plane," he said.

"You will have a contact at the Chateau," Ken said. "Here's his picture." He handed over an eight-by-ten glossy, black and white.

Grofield looked at a chubby-faced man with horn-rimmed glasses and a bushy mustache. He looked like the kind of cheerful suburban neighbor who borrows everybody's power mower. Grofield said, "My contact is a man? No beautiful girl?"

"Beautiful girls tend not to volunteer for this sort of work," Ken said.

Grofield looked at him. "You mean you two are volunteers?"

"As are you, friend," Charlie said. "Let's not lose sight of that."

"Let's not." Grofield handed Ken back the photo and said, "Do we have a secret handshake or something?"

"Why should you? You already know what he looks like, and he knows what you look like."

"How?"

"We sent him a blow-up from your picture in *Player's Guide*."

"Oh."

Ken said, "His name is Henry Carlson. Don't get in touch with him unless you have something specific to report, or a request to make or something like that."

"Okay."

"I don't suppose I have to point out," Ken went on, "that Henry won't be the only member of our organization in your vicinity for the next few days."

"There'll be others?"

"Oh yes."

"Do I get to look at their pictures?"

Ken smiled, not thinly. "Afraid not. You'll probably never have any contact with them at all."

"Unless," Charlie said, in a friendly way, "you decide to run out on us. Like during the layover in New York."

"Who, me?"

"We know you wouldn't," Charlie said. "It's our bosses, they don't trust anybody."

Ken tossed over a thick white envelope. "There's your money and tickets," he said. "The hotel room is already paid for."

Grofield tucked the envelope unopened in an inner pocket. "I suppose I thank you guys," he said. "For getting me out of that jam."

"Time will tell," Ken said.

∮

FOUR

∮

TWO HOURS LATE, Grofield's plane ovaled between massed gray clouds and the grubby sprawl of New York City. It was eight o'clock in the evening, and through snow and haze Grofield could look down at the monotonous crisscross rows of lights or up at the dull gray-red reflection of those lights on the underpart of the cloud bank. Neither prospect pleased.

In fact, no prospect at all was pleasing. Grofield had been looking forward to this plane not taking off at all, thereby maybe giving him some extra time to wiggle out of this mess, but the weather had unfortunately lifted, and so had the plane, and now here was New York. The Quebec plane would leave too, he was pessimistically sure of that, the Quebec plane would leave if it had to go north on the Thruway.

Who were his guards? The plane was half empty, but even so there were a good dozen men aboard who could conceivably be co-workers of Charlie and Ken. The damn thing was, intelligence agents were *supposed* to look like ordinary people, so the ones he'd picked out probably could all be eliminated. Once he'd decided an individual looked like a secret agent, by definition that person could not possibly *be* a secret agent. It was all very frustrating.

It was almost frustrating enough to make him give up and go along with their scenario. After all, even if he did elude them—in New York, say—they would surely not be the kind to forgive and forget. They would keep looking for him, and if they ever found him they would surely find some way to dump that armored car heist on him. So it would mean giving up his own name, it would mean joining Equity all over again with a new name—he'd have to grow a mustache, maybe, or change his hairstyle—it would mean giving up his small-time but satisfying acting career with the credits he'd amassed over the years and starting all over again, having to avoid as much as possible theaters and actors and directors who already knew him as Alan Grofield.

It would be a painful and frustrating and dangerous process, rebuilding a new life within the same very public career, but it would have one compelling advantage over playing Ken and Charlie's game: he would be alive. Whereas if he went to Quebec and started pussyfooting amid a lot of incognito colonels and generals, playing at foreign intrigue, a game he knew not at all, it seemed to him there was only one finish he could reasonably anticipate. His own. Better discommoded than dead.

The problem was, how to make his escape. It was tough to run away from people if you didn't know which people you were running away from. But he had to make the try.

In the meantime, the seat belt and smoking signs were lit, and the plane had finally quit ovaling and had started its long slanting approach, like coasting down an endless driveway. Outside the window, the dull red clouds were getting higher and higher, the grimy pinball machine below was getting closer and closer, then suddenly there were no lights at all down below, and then just a few stray lights, blue ones over there, one revolving yellow light, a few white dots in the snowy darkness, and all at once there was a feeling of how fast the plane was going. Then they hit, bumping hard, landing again, skid-swerving slightly, and Grofield put a hand to his seat belt, prepared to resist being killed by the airline too, but a second later he could feel the plane coming under control again, and he sat back in the seat and looked out at the distant small lights of Kennedy Airport. The plane braked, the engines roaring, and then became tame, and for the next ten minutes they trundled back and forth in the outfield, making lefts and rights seemingly at random, the lights of the low buildings never seeming to get any closer, and then for no reason at all they stopped. Grofield looked across the aisle and out the window on the other side, and there was the terminal building.

The aisle became crowded. Grofield carried his overcoat over his arm and inched off the plane with everybody else. No one seemed to pay him any particular attention.

Inside the terminal building, an endless, broad, cream-colored corridor led to a row of glass doors, beyond which Grofield found himself suddenly face to face with a short, beaming man wearing a black overcoat and a hat with a plastic raincover on it. The beaming man said, "Mr. Grofield! Have a pleasant flight?"

Grofield looked at him. "Do I know you?"

"I'm a friend of Ken's," the beaming man said. "Call me Murray."

"Hello, Murray."

"You sound depressed. Rough flight?"

"That must be it," Grofield said.

"A hell of a day to fly. Well, let's go get your luggage."

They went and got the luggage, which Murray insisted on carrying. They then went and stood by the glass exit doors to wait for the terminal bus. "The last report I got," Murray said, "is that your Quebec plane will take off, but it'll be about an hour late."

"Well, that's a relief," Grofield said.

"I thought we'd have dinner in the International Arrivals Building," Murray said. "Unless you already ate on the plane."

"I didn't eat much," Grofield said. "Is the government buying?"

"The least we can do," Murray said happily.

"You're damn right," Grofield said.

Murray said, "We'll just check you in over at Northways, give them the suitcase, and then go over and eat."

"Wonderful."

That was what they did, traveling twice on the terminal bus, the second time getting off at the International Arrivals Building and taking the escalator to the second-floor restaurant the Brass Rail operates there under the name Golden Door. The restaurant was nearly empty, probably because of the snow. They were shown to a table, they ordered drinks, and Grofield said, "I'll just go wash up."

"Of course," Murray said. "We have plenty of time."

"Right," Grofield said, and went off to the men's room but not inside. Looking through banks of artificial foliage, he watched until he was sure Murray was looking the other way, and then unchecked his overcoat and hurried down the stairs.

There would be at least one other, he already knew that. But would they try to stop him, or merely follow him? If they tried to stop him, he would have to try and get away.

But no one came near him. He hurried out of the building, shrugging his overcoat on, and there were half a dozen cabs huddled in the snow against the curb there. He got into the lead cab and said, "Manhattan."

"Certainly," said the driver.

With the snow, it was impossible to tell if he was being followed, but he assumed he was. He sat back in the cab and tried to relax for a while.

There wasn't very much traffic, but what there was moved very slowly. The snow was coming down in large, lazy, wet clumps, the street was gray slush streaked with black tire tracks. Grofield's cab threaded the maze out of the airport and took the Van Wyck Expressway toward Manhattan. After they crossed the Belt Parkway the traffic was stop and go. They rode a good twenty minutes before Grofield leaned forward and pointed to an overpass just ahead of them, saying, "Is that Jamaica Avenue?"

"Right."

Grofield handed over two dollars. "I'll get out here," he said.

The driver looked at him in astonishment. "In the middle of the. highway?"

"Everything's okay," Grofield said. The line of traffic was stopped at that point, so he opened the left-hand door and stepped out into the snow. He shut the door again, saw the driver gaping through his side window at him like a goldfish in his bowl, and walked around the cab and between cars to the right side of the road. He didn't have overshoes, and wet snow was already down inside his shoes, trickling inside his socks.

He went up the steep snowy slope, slipping and sliding, going to his knees a couple of times, getting his bare hands cold and wet in the snow, but when he got to the top and looked back there was no one coming up after him. He turned away and walked up to Jamaica Avenue and turned right to Queens Boulevard and the subway entrance. He had a ten-minute wait for a train, and couldn't tell if anyone on the platform with him was paying him any particular attention. He rode the train fourteen stops to Eastern Parkway, got off, walked aimlessly around that sprawling station, could find no one following him, and took a Canarsie Line train on into Manhattan, changing at Union Square for the Lexington Avenue train uptown. Again, nobody seemed to be following him. He rode up to Grand Central, left the subway, went upstairs to the railroad terminal, and bought a ticket on a train to Albany, leaving in ten minutes. He bought a newspaper and sat in a corner of the terminal with the paper up in front of his face for seven minutes, until someone said, "Shall we go back, Mr. Grofield?"

He lowered the paper, and looked up at two hefty types in windbreakers and cloth caps. They didn't look at all cheery or friendly, and he'd never seen either of them before in his life. He said, "I'm sorry, you must be mistaking me for someone else."

"Murray doesn't want to order before you get back," one of them said. "So why don't we start back now?"

"I really don't know what you're talking about," Grofield said.

The other one said, "Grofield, you aren't going to get away from us. But if you want to play hide and seek a while, we'll go along. You've got a little over two hours before plane time. We'll give you thirty minutes' head start if you want, and we'll still pick you up in plenty of time to catch the plane. Now, do you want to run around in the snow for two hours, or do you want to go have dinner with Murray?"

Grofield stared at them. How could they do it? How could they find him so easily? How could they make a challenge like that? Was it a bluff? Somehow he doubted it.

So what now? Run? Fight? Grofield looked at them, at their faces and their hands and their shoulders, and he sighed and folded his paper and got to his feet. "Let's not keep Murray waiting," he said.

FIVE

MURRAY PUT DOWN his empty brandy glass and made a lazy smile of contentment. "Now," he said, "that was delicious. Mr. Grofield, you have made me a very happy man. If only all my assignments could be like this one."

Grofield had refused an after-dinner drink, and was frowning over his third cup of coffee. He had been sullen throughout the meal, a fact Murray had managed somehow totally to ignore. Murray had told funny stories about New York City, he'd made delighted comments about the food, he'd delivered himself of animated monologues about air travel, and through it all Grofield had frowned and sulked, deep in gloomy thought. But now he looked across the table at Murray and said, "It's in the clothes."

Startled, Murray looked down at himself. "I did? Where?"

"It's somewhere in my clothes," Grofield said. "I knew there had to be an answer, and that's it."

Murray squinted at Grofield's chest. "I don't see anything."

"Some kind of radio transmitter," Grofield said thoughtfully, and looked off into space, thinking about it.

Murray said, "I'm sorry, I don't understand."

Grofield focused on him again. "I wasn't followed," he said. "I'm absolutely sure of that. From at least the time I left the cab, I wasn't followed. Nobody trailed me to Grand Central. So how come I was picked up there, that's what I've been trying to figure out."

Murray laid a finger beside his nose and winked, a Jewish Santa Claus. "We have our methods," he said.

"You're damn right you do," Grofield agreed. "And one of those storm troopers that picked me up offered me a thirty-minute head start, and he didn't give me the impression he was kidding. So I've been sitting here and I've been trying to figure out how you people could keep finding me without tailing me, and now I know how it's done."

"Very good!" Murray said. He seemed proud of Grofield's deductive abilities.

"You've put some sort of transmitter in my clothes," Grofield said. "Everything I'm wearing came from you people, except my shoes. With today's miniaturization, with printed circuits—"

"Painted circuits," Murray said.

"Painted?"

"Certainly. Metallic paint can be used in place of wiring, it's in very common practice."

"So that's even smaller," Grofield said. "Somewhere in a lining, in a seam, somewhere in my clothing there's a tiny transmitter. All you need is two mobile receivers and you can home in on me anywhere."

"That's very interesting," Murray said. He looked and sounded like an unconcerned spectator considering an interesting theory. "But it wouldn't have to be in your clothing," he said.

"Where else could it be?"

"Well, you were in the hospital for a few days, I understand."

"What?" Grofield stared at him in horror. "Inside my *body*? A transmitter under my *skin*?"

Murray grinned impishly. "I'm just teasing," he said. "We wouldn't do a thing like that."

"My God!" Grofield said. He felt physically weak. "What a thing even to think about!"

Murray looked thoughtful. "But, you know," he said slowly, "that isn't such a bad idea. You take your known Commie, say, or your incorrigible criminal, like you, for instance, you take whoever it might be you're interested in, you put the little transmitter in them, then any time you wanted to know what they were up to you'd just triangulate on them, see where they were, go on over and check them out."

"That's the most evil thing I ever heard in my life," Grofield said.

"Why?" Murray seemed honestly puzzled. "We wouldn't use it on *good* people," he said. "Just *bad* people." He smiled broadly, delighted with himself. "You know what I'm going to do? I'm going to put that in the suggestion box back in the office."

Grofield looked at him. "I keep having the strong feeling," he said, "that for the sake of generations unborn I ought to strangle you here and now."

Murray chuckled, not taking him seriously. "Oh, you," he said. "You've just got a vested interest, that's all. Being a thief and everything."

Grofield kept looking at him, but just as Murray was beginning to get uncomfortable Grofield shook his head. "It wouldn't be any use," he said. "No army can withstand the strength of an idea whose time has come."

Murray was interested. "You think so? That's a nice phrase."

"They come to me," Grofield said. "Should we go get the plane?"

Murray looked at his watch. "Right you are!" he said, and began waving his Diners Club card for the check.

$\mathcal{S}$

SIX

$\mathcal{S}$

GROFIELD PLUCKED A DOLLAR BILL from his wallet, but it had a man's face on it so he put it back. He selected another, and it had a woman's face on it, and he nodded in satisfaction. Also the greens were brighter, the serial number was in red and the design was different. Finally, it said on it in large letters CANADA. That was good enough for Grofield, which meant it was good enough for the bellboy. Grofield gave it to him, the bellboy knuckled his brow and said, "Zheh," which is French for monsieur, and then he went away, shut the door, left Grofield alone.

Grofield yawned. After a while his jaw began to ache, but the yawn wouldn't stop. Would the hinge break, would he spend the rest of his life with his jaw dangling down on his chest? How could he deliver lines that way? Grofield reeled around, trying to stop yawning, and at last the pressure eased and his aching mouth slowly closed, like a theater door.

It was five minutes to eight in the morning. The plane from New York hadn't loaded until nearly 1 A.M., and then hadn't taken off until after three. Grofield had napped for about half an hour before the plane got into the air, but once aloft sleep had been impossible. God, having died, had apparently been reincarnated as a basketball player and had dribbled the plane all the way to Quebec. Somewhere along the way the snow and clouds and general storminess had faded away, leaving only the frisky wind to play with the plane like a kitten with a crumpled cigarette package, and the stewardesses had spent most of the flight rushing up and down the aisle with air sickness bags, empty in one direction, full in the other.

They had descended at last on Quebec at first light, like a plague ship, and Grofield had been mildly surprised when the airport officials had allowed them to debark. The stewardess at the exit had been glassy-eyed as she'd given each passenger the ritual, "Good to have you aboard," and Grofield had decided not to respond.

The cab driver had been surly, though *he* hadn't been on that plane. It was a twelve-mile trip from airport to hotel, all of it southeast, directly into the just-risen sun, and Grofield had spent most of it with his hands over his eyes. They'd come at the Chateau Frontenac from the west, the undramatic side, but drama would have been wasted on him this morning anyway. The process of transferring himself and suitcase from cab to hotel room was a complicated one, but ritualized, so it was possible to do it without thinking about it, and he did, and now at last he was here.

There were things to do, of course. He had to buy new clothing, without electronics. He had to reconnoiter the hotel, and then the city. He had to figure out the best way to get out of this part of the world without being intercepted. Lots of things to do, all important, all necessary, and he was going to definitely do them. Definitely. But not yet.

Sleep. First there had to be some sleep. In his present condition Grofield doubted he could successfully evade a paraplegic with a flat tire. Rest and recuperation were first on the agenda, and once he was reasonably alert once more he could get on with his escape plans. In the meantime, sleep.

And before sleep, a shower. The events of the last fifteen hours, the traveling and the running around New York City in a snowstorm and all, had left him not only exhausted but also very grimy and a nervous wreck. He was probably too tense to lose consciousness at the moment, no matter how badly he needed sleep, and a shower would do a lot to correct that, as well as making it possible for him to stand being around himself.

So he took a shower, leaving a trail of clothing from the middle of the bedroom into the bathroom, and standing in the hot spray with head and shoulders and jaw all drooping until he felt the tension draining away, felt his eyelids getting heavy instead of grainy, knew that now he could sleep. Oh, yeah, now he could sleep.

He got out of the shower, toweled himself dry, and walked nude into the room, stopping short in the doorway. Seated on the chair across the room was a coal black Negro girl in a green pants suit, looking like Robin Hood got up for a Commando raid. She looked Grofield up and down and said, as though to herself, "They are smaller."

"I don't believe it," Grofield said.

"Take my word for it," she said.

"I don't believe God could be so cruel," Grofield said. "All I want to do is sleep. I don't want anything complicated now."

"Nothing complicated," the girl said briskly. Behind her camouflage she was a stunning girl, with large flashing eyes and close-cropped hair in the natural style, very wooly. She spoke with a vaguely British accent. She said, "All you have to do is tell me who sent you here and why. Then I'll go away and you can sleep."

"My doctor," Grofield said. "For the waters."

"What?"

"My doctor sent me here. For the waters."

"What waters?" She sounded more annoyed than confused.

"I was misinformed," Grofield said. "Humphrey Bogart and Claude Rains, *Casablanca*, 1942. I hope you have an exit line, because you're exiting." He walked toward the bed.

Now she was more confused than annoyed. "What the hell are you talking about?"

"How do I know? I'm asleep." He pulled the spread off the bed and dumped it on the floor.

"Look, you," she said, and pointed a finger at him. "*I'm* asking nice. You don't answer me, the next one who shows up won't be so easy to get along with."

Grofield slid between the delicious crisp sheets. "Be sure the door is locked when you go out," he said, and collapsed backward onto the pillow.

"Hey," she said. "Hey!"

Grofield's eyes closed, and whatever else she might have said was drowned out by the whirring of the wings of Morpheus.

SEVEN

SOMEWHERE A LIGHT WAS BURNING, making a dull red glow on Grofield's eyelids. He came very slowly up toward consciousness, aware of the red glow for a long while before being aware that he was awake, and then continuing to lie there for another period of time after he was awake, thinking about who he was and where he was and all of the things that had happened in his recent history and what was he going to do about it all and also he was very very hungry.

He didn't want to open his eyes, because the light would blind him, and it took him a long while to decide what to do instead. At last he rolled over onto his other side, keeping his eyes squeezed shut as he moved, and when the red glow cut off he opened his eyes, and found he was facing the window, which was heavily draped. The source of the light was somewhere in this room.

A page turned. A very distinctive sound, the sound of a page turning. Page of a book.

Was she still here, waiting for him to wake up? How long had she been sitting here, for God's sake? What time was it? He struggled his left arm up from under the covers and the wrist was naked, of course, his watch being on the shelf over the sink in the bathroom.

He was very very hungry.

Another page turned.

He didn't want another session with that girl now, he really didn't. He was going to have to be firm, that's all, get rid of her and no nonsense. Make an appointment with her for later on, if she insisted. During business hours.

He steeled himself for the effort, rolled over onto his back, sat up, and looked into the mild eyes of Henry Carlson, who said, "So you're awake."

"I know you," Grofield said.

"Ken showed you my picture. And of course I've seen yours. Tell me, was it retouched?"

What hurt was that the question didn't seem to be malicious. Henry Carlson looked honestly and innocently interested in the answer. Grumpily Grofield said, "Of course not."

"Oh. No offense."

"I'm just not at my best in the morning."

"Hardly morning," Carlson said, and looked at his watch. "Three twenty-five." Disapprovingly he added, "In the afternoon."

"Us counterspies work funny hours."

Carlson got very prim. "That's not a good sort of joke, you know."

"It isn't?"

Carlson could be seen making an effort to be friendly with the lower orders. "Before we go any farther, Alan—may I call you Alan?"

"No," Grofield said, and got out of bed, and stomped away to the bathroom.

When he came out again ten minutes later, shaved and shiny and much more awake, he was still naked and Carlson was still sitting in the same chair under the same lit floor lamp with the same hardcover book open in his lap. Carlson looked at Grofield and got fidgety. "I suppose actors get used to ignoring usual conventions of modesty," he said, and tried a friendly smile that didn't entirely work.

Grofield, crossing to his suitcase, glanced at Carlson and said, "I suppose secret agents get used to ignoring the usual conventions of politeness. Like not coming into rooms uninvited."

Carlson's face grew troubled. "Aren't we going to get along? I was hoping everything would be friendly."

"I bet you were." Grofield opened the suitcase and started dressing. "Excuse me while I put on my radio," he said.

"I beg your pardon?"

"Never mind. Was this just a social call or did you have a motive?"

"Miss Kamdela," Carlson said.

Grofield stopped with one pant leg on. "Say again?"

"Miss Vivian Kamdela," Carlson said.

Grofield put his other foot in the other pant leg and pulled his trousers up. "I bet," he said, "that's the black lady who was in here this morning."

"Well, of course. You seemed to be on very good terms with her." Carlson was being prim again.

"Sure," Grofield said. "We skipped over the part where you exchange names, that's all."

"What did she want?"

"To know who sent me and why. And if she hung around to watch you come in here, she probably no longer has to ask." Grofield carried his tie into the bathroom and put it on in front of the mirror.

Carlson called from the other room, "No one saw me come in, I guarantee it. Why did she want to know about you?"

"She didn't say." The tie came the right length on the first try, a rare occurrence. A straw in the wind, or a sign that his luck was changing? He patted the tie against his shirt front and walked back out to the other room. "Shall we have breakfast together or are we making believe we have security to maintain?"

"It is hardly make-believe," Carlson said stiffly. "A great deal of care has been put into this operation, to be absolutely certain no one knows of our connection with you."

"Then how come Miss Whatsername . . ."

"Vivian Kamdela."

"Right. How come she showed up to ask questions?"

"That's what I'm here to find out."

"You're zigging when you should be zagging. Go ask Miss Vivian Whosis."

"Kamdela."

"All right, Kamdela." Struck by a sudden thought, Grofield said, "Is she African?"

"Of course."

"Not from Undurwa, by any chance?"

"Are you merely pretending ignorance, Mr. Grofield?"

"No more than you are, Mr. Carlson. A fellow named Onum Marba is one of my two acquaintances at this meeting I'm supposed to crash. He comes from Undurwa. If he saw me this morning when I checked in, it might have made him curious to know if it was just coincidence. He has a very dry sense of humor, Marba has, it would be his kind of thing to send a girl around to ask the questions."

"I see," Carlson said thoughtfully. "That does make sense."

"You noticed."

"It was all I wanted to know, really. Why Miss Kamdela was here." He closed his book and got to his feet. It was *The Espionage Establishment*, by David Wise and Thomas B. Ross.

Grofield gestured at the book. "They give you a mention?"

"Happily, no."

"Better luck next time. You want to join me for breakfast?"

"At this hour?"

"I'll call what I eat breakfast, you call yours whatever you want. You coming?"

"No, Mr. Grofield. There really is security to maintain, you know, it isn't all a joke. If your cover is blown, you realize, you won't be any further use to us at all. I don't know exactly what my superiors would want to do about you in such a case."

"Back into the frying pan, eh?"

"I beg your pardon?"

"Go ahead," Grofield said. "All right, how do you want to work this?"

"You go on out," Carlson told him, "and I'll leave a few minutes after you."

"Why don't we do it the other way around? You first."

"If the representative from Undurwa is keeping you under observation, this room will now be watched. If you go out first, the watcher will leave with you, and I will be able to leave unobserved."

"Okay, that makes sense. But be sure the door is locked when you go out."

"Certainly."

"Not that it does any good," Grofield grumbled, and went away to find breakfast.

EIGHT

It is impossible to get breakfast at four o'clock in the afternoon. In fact, it's impossible to get any meal at all, it being too late for lunch and too early for dinner. Grofield finally settled for an over-done hamburger, oily french fries and a wilted salad, washed down with plenty of coffee, and afterward was sorry he'd broken his fast at all.

The next half hour he spent at Holt Renfrew, a department store near the hotel, where he spent most of his government-issue hundred dollars fitting himself out with a complete set of non-broadcasting apparel. He considered leaving the store in new clothing, leaving all of the old stuff behind and walking quietly away, but he doubted it could be done right now. If some of Carlson's friends weren't watching him, surely some of Marba's friends were. The thing to do was wait at the hotel until tonight, slip out under cover of darkness. So he left the store wearing the same clothes he'd worn in.

Going out the narrow door, carrying his package, he was bumped into by a man hurrying in, and there was a sudden sting on his left arm where he was bumped against. Maybe the man's cuff link had sharp edges. Grofield looked after him in irritation, then went on out to the sidewalk and fell on his face.

He didn't lose consciousness, that was the worst part of it, he just had no strength any more, no connection to any part of his body. His eyes had closed reflexively when he'd fallen, and were still closed, but he could hear the voices all around him and he could feel the new pains in his knees and left shoulder and nose, where he'd hit the concrete.

The voices around him were being startled, and then concerned. Hands touched him, people foolishly asked him questions such as "Are you all right?" He thought, *If I were all right, I wouldn't be lying here in the middle of the sidewalk,* but it was impossible to say it. Impossible to say or do anything.

"I'm a doctor," said a new voice, with a French accent, or more probably a French-Canadian accent. Hands, firm but gentle, rolled him over onto his back. A thumb lifted his eyelid and he found himself looking up at vague shapes. He couldn't focus, he couldn't get any of the shapes to come in clearly.

The doctor was touching him, checking his pulse, patting his chest, feeling his forehead, and finally he said, "This man has had an epileptic fit."

Grofield wanted to frown. An epileptic fit? He didn't have epilepsy, this doctor was a buffoon. But there was no way to tell him so.

The doctor was saying, "We must get him to a hospital at once. Does anyone have an auto handy?"

"I do, Doctor, right over here."

"Good. If some of you would help lift him . . ."

Grofield was lifted and borne away. Inside, his mind was still churning around, trying to figure things out. He hadn't had an epileptic fit, this doctor had made a maybe understandable but definitely wrong diagnosis. Could his breakfast have had this severe an effect on him? Impossible.

The man who'd bumped into him. The sting on the arm. He'd been poisoned!

Good God! How much time did he have? Somebody would have to make the right diagnosis fast, if he was to be given the antidote. If there was an antidote.

There was a great deal of difficulty getting him into the car. They kept bumping parts of him against metal, shouting advice into each other's ear, tugging him back out and starting all over again. Somebody even said, "Do you think we should wait for an ambulance?"

No no, thought Grofield, and the doctor's voice echoed his sentiment, saying, "No, no. There is a certain urgency in cases like this."

You betcha, thought Grofield, and with a final scraping heave they at last got him into the car, where he felt himself sprawled across the rear set. His legs were bundled in after him, like piles of laundry, and the door slammed.

After that it was all very fast. Car doors opened, and Grofield heard the doctor saying, apparently to the bystanders, "I'll go along to the hospital." There were murmurs of approval, and then the car jounced as people got into it, and then doors slammed. Grofield heard the engine start, felt the car back up, go forward, back up again, and at last begin to move steadily forward.

Grofield's one still-open eye could see two round vague shapes, the heads of the driver and the doctor. Good Samaritans. Maybe Canadians were friendlier than people in the States.

The driver said, "How is he?"

The doctor said, "He's all right. The overcoat gave you no difficulty?"

"None. It went right through the sleeve, just as you said."

"You see? Sometimes I do know what I'm talking about."

Grofield's open eye was burning for lack of moisture. He hadn't been blinking, it seemed as though he couldn't blink, and it was beginning to get painful, distracting him from thinking about what they were saying up front. What would happen if his eye dried out completely?

Through the sleeve?

The driver was the one who'd poisoned him!

The doctor's head turned and he grunted, saying, "Um. That's no good." Something like a cloud came at Grofield's face, a thumb touched his eyelid, closed it down over his eye, left him alone with his thoughts.

They weren't happy thoughts. The fact that he had given up the warmth and security of a long prison sentence for all this was particularly displeasing. He could be in prison right now, reading a magazine, smoking a cigarette, idly wondering what movie he would be shown tonight, instead of lying poisoned in the back of some stranger's car, probably on his way to a shallow grave somewhere.

He couldn't move. He strained and strained, but he couldn't so much as flex a muscle. The car jounced along, and he felt himself flopping on the back seat like a Raggedy Andy doll, and he didn't know whether he wanted most to be terrified or enraged, so he was both.

It was frightening to die, and more so to die in darkness, among strangers, and foolishly. And it was infuriating to die foolishly, needlessly, caught up in other people's intrigues.

Still, terror is stronger than fury, and by the time the car came to a stop at last Grofield was in near-panic. If he could have run, he would have run. If he could have begged, he would have begged. If he could have wept, he would have wept.

Hands touched him. He could feel, his senses were all in perfect working order, it was only somehow the chain of command from his mind to his body that had been broken down. He was helpless, but aware, the worst possible state.

He was dragged from the car, not very gently. Were they going to bury him alive? The fright that gave him was enough to drag from him a small moan, so small and high-pitched as to redouble his terror. Had that been *his* voice?

He was carried somewhere, jounced along uneven ground, then indoors. The pacing of his carriers was smoother, and he could hear the sound of their feet on the wooden floor.

He was dropped on something, something soft and scratchy, like an old sofa. He wished he could see, he wished he could open his eyes, and in straining to open them it seemed as though he did crack the lids just a little. A line of light seeped in, but not enough for him to really see anything.

A new voice said, "So you got him."

"No trouble at all." That was the doctor.

"How long before we can question him?"

"Not long. Perhaps ten minutes. He's started to come around already."

The thumb abruptly slid up his eyelid again, and Grofield could see. A face was leaning over him, studying him. Grofield could focus better now, could see that the face was middle-aged and heavy-jowled, with a bushy black mustache. The face said, "Yes. Maybe sooner." It was the doctor.

The new voice said, "You weren't followed?" Unlike the doctor and the driver, he didn't have a French-Canadian accent, though his words were accented. A harsher echo than French, though. German? Not exactly.

The doctor's thumb slid Grofield's eyelid closed again, and from the sound of his voice he had turned and was walking away. "Of course we weren't followed. Albert knows how to do those things." He pronounced the name the French way, Al Bear, a character in a book for children.

Grofield could have kissed them all, Al Bear and the doctor and the new voice, kissed them and hugged them and handed out cigars. He wasn't going to die! They weren't going to kill him! It was only a temporary paralysis, only a thing they'd done to bring him here without a lot of fuss so they could ask him questions.

Ask away! Such inane gratitude did he feel, he would tell them anything. He was alive, they could ask whatever they wanted. What business was all this of his anyway? Ask, ask! He was impatient for the effects of the drug to wear off, so he could start answering questions.

In the meantime, the voices had moved farther away and he

could no longer make out what they were saying. They were still in the same room, but a distance away and speaking softly. They undoubtedly understood that he could hear them, that he was conscious, and they probably had private things they wanted to say to one another. That was all right, that was understandable, he wasn't offended by anything like that. He was alive, wasn't he?

He certainly was, and his body was beginning to tell him so. His joints had started to tingle, the way frostbitten fingers do when they're starting to warm up. But the tingle now wasn't in his fingertips, it was in his elbows and knees and shoulders and ankles and wrists, in his knuckles and neck and crotch, in all the joints of his body, a tingling that was getting worse and worse. Life was coming back, all right, with a vengeance.

He moaned. It wasn't planned, he would have preferred to stay quiet, but instead he moaned. And from across the room heard the doctor say, "Ah, here he comes now." The sound increasing as though he was walking this way. "Are you back with us, Mr. Grofield?"

There were three shots. Somebody yelled. Somebody else cursed. A crashing sound might have been a door giving way. More shots. Something puffed into the sofa cushion near his left ear. There were screams and shouts and shots and running feet. A high-pitched yell was followed by a ba-*dump*, as though someone had fallen, heavily.

There was nothing Grofield could do but lie there. He swore an oath to himself that if ever he got the control of his body back he would punch the mouths of the first ten men he saw. Enough was enough, dammit!

His eyes opened. The lids lifted slowly, reluctantly, but they did lift, and he saw a large rustic room full of moose heads and fireplaces and scratchy-looking furniture. There was a smell of gunpowder in the air. The room, so far as he could see, was vacant, the shooting and shouting having moved somewhere into the distance. Far away, doors slammed, people yelled. An automobile raced away, squealing rubber.

Grofield moved his hands, small vague movements that went nowhere and did no one any good. He struggled to re-establish contact with his legs, and was finally rewarded with an increase in the tingling pain in his knees. Everything was stinging as though he'd been bitten all over by a million bees.

But the legs were moving. Slowly, very slowly, but moving. He slid them leftward, away from the sofa back, toward the floor, and was rewarded at last with a thump as his left foot dropped off the edge and hit the floor. The right leg moved more slowly, but at last it too cleared the edge and drooped floorward, though his position didn't let it reach all the way.

With every second now, his physical shape was improving. The drug, whatever it was, was wearing off more and more rapidly. The stinging and tingling was easing, too.

Could he sit up? He moved his arms some more, not effectively, then took hold of the top of the sofa back in both hands and slowly pulled himself upward. There was one bad instant of no balance, a sort of threshold between lying and sitting, but he struggled past that point and there he was sitting up.

He was resting a second before trying the major operation of standing when a door to the right opened and three men walked in with drawn guns in their hands. None of them was the doctor.

Grofield looked at them, too worn out even to wonder what this bunch had in mind for him. In the middle of the floor a man was lying on his face, and across the way a door hung broken from its hinges, exposing a view of wintry mountains. Grofield had no way of knowing where he was or who anybody was or what anybody wanted. He had never been so helpless in his life, and was tending to react to it by simply giving up, on the basis that if it won't do any good to struggle, don't struggle.

One of the three men went directly to the gaping front door, the second went to the man lying on the floor, and the third came over to Grofield. Grofield looked up at him and was astonished to see it was Ken.

Ken said, "You all right?"

"Drugged," Grofield said. "Wearing off."

"Good." He put his gun away and walked over to the second man, who was a stranger to Grofield, not Charlie. "How's this one?" he asked.

"Dead," the stranger said. He'd taken the dead man's wallet and was leafing through it. "Driver's license," he said. "Made out to Albert Beaudry." He pronounced Albert the English way.

"Don't know that name," Ken said. "Let's see his face."

The stranger rolled the dead man onto his back, and they both studied his face a minute. "New to me," the stranger said.

"Me too," Ken said. He looked over at the doorway, but the third man—also not Charlie—had gone on outside, so he turned to Grofield instead. "You strong enough to stand?"

"I don't know."

"Did you get a good look at this guy before?"

"I didn't get a good look at anybody. I've been out of it since they got hold of me."

Ken shook his head. "You'll never know," he said, "how much I dislike working with amateurs."

"Fire me," Grofield said. "Go ahead, I can take it."

"Forget it, Grofield. Come over here and see do you recognize this guy."

"We used to be on a first-name basis, you and I," Grofield said, trying to struggle to his feet.

The stranger came over and helped Grofield up, holding onto his arm so he wouldn't fall over again. Ken said, "That was back when you were acting cooperative. Come over here."

Grofield and the stranger weaved over there, and Grofield looked down at the face of the dead man. "He bumped into me on my way out of Holt Renfrew," he said. "That's when he drugged me."

"Did you ever see him before?"

"No."

"Did you hear them talking at all?"

"Sure. I was never really out, just paralyzed."

"Did you hear anything to tell you who they work for, what they wanted?"

"Nothing. Just that they wanted to question me."

"Did they question you?"

"They didn't get around to it. You people showed up too soon."

Ken nodded, looking grumpy, and glanced around the room. "Whose package is that?"

It was what Grofield had just bought, full of the new clothing, and it was standing now against the wall near the broken door. Grofield looked at it and said, "I don't know. Theirs, I guess."

"You're a lousy liar, Grofield," Ken said. "It's yours. You were planning a runout."

"Who says it's mine?"

The stranger holding his arm grinned and said, "I do, pal. I watched you buy it."

Grofield looked at him. "Oh," he said, then flared up, saying, "If you were tailing me like that, how come you let those guys take me away?"

"I wasn't tailing you," the stranger said. "I dropped into the store to see what you were doing. Once I saw, I left again."

"We were waiting for you to make your move," Ken said. "We were gonna give you a little rope, then reel you in."

"You people are sadistic."

"We just want you to understand," Ken told him, "that you're with us for the duration." He pointed a finger at Grofield. "You make any more moves toward running out on us, Grofield, we'll pack you up and ship you back home to stand trial on that armored car job."

Grofield shrugged. "All right. You've got me sewn up."

"That's right. Let's go back to the hotel."

"Okay."

They started out, the stranger still helping Grofield stay upright, and Grofield said, "What about my package?"

"Leave it," Ken said. "We'd rather you wore what we gave you."

"Yeah, I guess you would."

"It's for your own protection," the stranger said cheerfully. "If you'd had those other duds on, we'd never have rescued you."

"Rescued me," Grofield said. "So this is what it's like to be rescued."

They led him out to the car.

NINE

THERE WAS NO WAY out of it. Grofield spent the long half hour of the ride back to Quebec thinking about that, learning reluctantly to accept it. There was no way out, he was going to have to try to get the information Ken and his buddies wanted, and at the same time keep that other bunch from kidnapping him again, and at the same time keep Marba and General Pozos from finding out he was actually working for the American government. A juggling act, that's what he was going to have to perform, simply because there was just no way out of it. They had him in a cage.

The third man was driving, with the stranger beside him, and Ken in back with Grofield. Nobody did much talking until they were back in the city of Quebec again, this time coming in from the northeast, having traveled down out of bleak and snowy mountains north of the city. As the buildings of the city began to fill in the spaces around them, Ken said, "Have you met Henry Carlson yet?"

"He was in my room when I woke up. He wanted to know why Vivian Kamdela had been to see me."

Ken looked sharply at him. "She went to see you?"

Grofield told Ken the history of his day, and when he was done Ken said, "All right, that's good, that gives you a way in. She'll be back, or others will come instead. You can't let them know you know they work for Colonel Rahgos . . ."

"I do?"

"President of Undurwa," Ken reminded him. "Your friend Marba's country."

"Oh. Right."

"What you do is, you insist on talking to their boss. Sooner or later they'll take you to Marba, and from there on you can ad-lib."

"I prefer working from a script, but all right."

"In the meantime, we'll try to find out who that bunch was that put the arm on you."

"That'd be nice."

"And keep them from doing it again."

"That'd be nicer."

They arrived at the hotel a few minutes later, but did not drive on in. Instead, they parked on the Place d'Armes. The short winter twilight had settled on the city now, and across the way the Chateau Frontenac was dramatically lit in amber and green.

Ken said, "We'll check out your room first, just in case they're waiting for you. You take a walk around the block and then go on in."

"All right."

The effects of the drug had mostly worn off by now, but Grofield was still a little shaky when he stepped out of the car. The cold air slapped his face, waking him up and making him dizzy at the same time

The stranger said, "You okay?"

"I'll do until the real thing comes along."

"That's the stuff."

"I bet it is."

Grofield tottered away, and had a boring walk past open restaurants and closed stores on Rue Sainte Anne, Rue des Jardins, Rue Buade, Rue du Trésor and back to Rue Sainte Anne again. By then he was more than ready to cross the Place d'Armes and go on into the hotel.

He didn't know if anyone paid attention to him in the lobby or not. He didn't really care. He simply walked over to a waiting elevator, told the uniformed boy, "Three," and was taken up to the third floor. He walked tiredly down the long hall to his room, reflecting that he'd been out of bed less than three hours and was already exhausted again, and fumbled with the key until he got the door open.

He went in and the lights were on. Henry Carlson was sitting in the same chair as before, slouching, his book open on his chest. Ken was at the telephone, and had turned to stare in disbelief at Grofield.

Grofield said, "Did I come back too soon?"

"I wouldn't have believed it," Ken said, and cradled the phone. He came quickly across the room toward Grofield, his face twisted with rage. "You son of a bitch, you had the gall to come back!"

Carlson wasn't moving. A hilt jutted out of the middle of the book. The book had been stuck to his chest with a knife. Carlson wasn't ever going to move again.

Grofield looked from Carlson to Ken and saw Ken's fist coming at his face.

TEN

GROFIELD CLOSED HIS LEFT HAND around the wrist just past Ken's
fist, made a half turn to the left, threw his right hand up against
the underpart of Ken's elbow to keep it locked, made a further
half turn leftward, doubled over, levered Ken's arm down toward
the floor, and the momentum of Ken's punch carried his body up
and over Grofield and through the middle of the air and into the
door, slamming it shut.

Grofield kept hold of the wrist, and used it to flip Ken onto his
back. He put one knee on Ken's chest, bent Ken's arm in on itself
to where it wasn't quite breaking, and touched a finger of his
other hand to a point on Ken's throat. "If I hit you there very
hard," he said, "you'll stop breathing."

Ken said nothing. He was breathing hard and his eyes watched
Grofield without blinking.

Grofield said, "If I killed Carlson, I will now kill you."

Ken still said nothing. His mouth was still twisted in a grimace
of exertion, or maybe of pain.

Grofield tapped Ken's throat with his fingertip. He waited a
few seconds more to be sure the message had sunk in, and then

quickly released Ken and got to his feet, moving back out of range.

Ken sat up slowly, rubbing his arm. "I don't know," he said, sullen and reluctant. "You're the natural for it."

"Why?"

"You were trying to run out on us. You bought new clothes, you were getting set to welsh on our deal. Henry was your watchdog here, so you killed him."

"If they're all as bright as you down there in Washington," Grofield said, "I'll put my money on the Third World. Ignoring the fact that it would be stupid and unnecessary for me to kill Henry at any time, and that I try whenever possible to avoid doing the stupid and the unnecessary, ignoring that for just a second, let me assure you that if I *was* going to kill Henry I wouldn't do it before I bought the new clothing, I'd do it afterward. Would I leave a corpse in my hotel room, where any passing maid could see it and leave me with no place to change clothes?"

"Maybe you let something slip. That you were going to run out."

"I don't let things slip," Grofield said.

"Damn it, Grofield, he's in your room!"

"Exactly where I left him. I told you he came to see me, and he wanted me to leave first so he wouldn't be spotted going out."

Ken sat there on the floor, rubbing his arm and frowning at the body across the room. "I don't know," he said again.

"Well, I do," Grofield said. "Maybe Honeybunch Kamdela came back and Henry threw a pass at her and she protected her honor."

Ken glowered at Grofield. "That's in pretty poor taste, Grofield," he said.

"Sometimes," Grofield said, "I find you hard to believe. You're such an oaf. I'll go out and circulate for a while, and when I come back I'll expect you and your friend to be out of here."

"Just a minute!" Ken struggled to his feet, favoring the bad arm. "You've got to help."

"The hell I do. I'm a specialist." Grofield headed for the door.

Ken blocked his way. "What if I walk out, and let you explain the body by yourself? It'll be found sooner or later."

"It has occurred to me," Grofield said, "that I am too valuable for that. At the moment, in this particular situation, I am the irreplaceable man. You can't get along without me. Therefore, you will protect me, you will see to it I am not bothered by police investigations, you will get your friend out of here before I come back."

Ken backed against the door. "I was emotionally upset when you came in here," he said, "or I wouldn't have thrown that easy punch. I know a little something about self-defense too, you know."

"It's lucky for me you were too stupid to remember it. Move over, Ken, if we start to fight you could break the transmitter in my shorts."

Ken stared at him a few seconds longer, then said, "You won't help."

"You've got a small army here, you don't need me. What *your* problem is, you don't want the rest of the team to know one of their number's been bumped off. You get little morale problems like that often?"

"I hope you screw up, Grofield," Ken said. "I hope you screw up so bad I get the order to take you right back and turn you in for that armored car job."

"And let the Third World capture Peoria? Move over, Ken, I'm off to save my country from the pygmies."

Ken moved over. "You cynical bastard," he said.

Grofield stopped with his hand on the knob. "If I don't come back from this mission," he said dramatically, "I want you to tell the folks back home. Tell them to be on their guard. Tell them to—tell them to—*watch the skies!*"

He went out chuckling, and Ken slammed the door behind him.

ELEVEN

IN A CORNER OF THE LOBBY was sitting Miss Vivian Kamdela, in textures of black. Black leather boots disappearing up under a black suede mini skirt, a black turtleneck sweater showing under an open, fitted black Russian coat decorated at collar and cuffs and hem with fluffs of black fur. The smooth texture of black skin and the woolly texture of black hair completed an arrangement that was somehow simultaneously wildly erotic and heavily menacing. The men walking by the cul-de-sac where she sat alone and apparently oblivious had a tendency to stare at her and fall over suitcases.

Thanking God he wasn't a masochist, Grofield entered the cul-de-sac and sat down in the other short sofa facing her. "Hello again," he said.

She looked in his general vicinity, but not directly at him, and said nothing.

Grofield persisted. "I'm ready to talk," he said. "How about taking me to Marba?"

She looked away again. Her manner said that he did not exist.

"What's up?" Grofield said. "I'm here to talk."

This time she did look directly at him, eyes cold and impersonal. "You've made a mistake," she said. "We haven't met."

"We've met, Vivian," he said, and was pleased to see her eyes shift for a second at the sound of her name. "Not formally, maybe, but you did see a lot of me."

A thin smile briefly touched her mouth, but she repeated, "You've made a mistake."

"Not me," he said, and now he was getting irritated. "There've been mistakes, Vivian, but I haven't made them. Right now there's a murdered man in my room upstairs, and if you people did it you ought to start giving me some damn good reasons why I shouldn't blow the whistle on you."

"Blow the whistle?" The curtains were still drawn behind her eyes. "If you have things you think you should tell someone officially, it is your duty to do so."

"You aren't paying attention, honey," Grofield said. "I know what's happening here this weekend. I know everybody's here under assumed names, but I know who's who. I know General Pozos is here. I know your president, Colonel Rahgos, is here. I know Onum Marba is here. I don't know what name you're registered under, but your real name is Vivian Kamdela and you're with the mission from Undurwa. I tell you there's a dead man in my room, and *I'm* not taking the rap for it. Now do you take me to Marba or do I start making loud embarrassing noises?"

The curtains had lifted now, showing worry underneath. Her brow furrowed, she said, "What do you mean, a dead man?"

"By a dead man I mean a man who's dead. With a knife in him. Stabbed right through his textbook."

"I know nothing of that," she said. "We had nothing to do with that. I don't know what you're mixed up in, but . . ."

"I'm mixed up in the Third World, and all because I'm a friend of your friend Marba. I want to talk to somebody. Marba's my first choice, but the local authorities are a satisfactory substitution."

She was looking more and more worried. If she'd been the type to chew her nails she'd have been gnawing away by now, but she wasn't. All she did was sit there and look worried and also look as though she was thinking very hard.

Grofield sat back and let her think. He'd delivered his message to the messenger, now let the messenger decide to take it from there

She did, at last, leaning forward and saying, "I'm not sure what to do at this point. Will you wait here for one moment?"

"I'll wait for two moments. No more."

"I'll go and see," she said, and got to her feet and went away, the black leather boots flashing below the fur-fringed black coat. Two men moving by in opposite directions walked into one another, gave perfunctory apologies without looking at one another, and drifted on.

Grofield sat back and waited. Whenever he stopped like this, his attention no longer required outside himself, he became aware again of the aftereffects of the drug he'd been given. His joints still ached and tingled slightly, a faint echo of the first pain he'd felt on coming out of the paralysis, and his nerves were a little jumpy, not as though he were nervous but as though he'd had too much coffee to drink. There didn't seem to be any real physical impairment, just the slight reminiscent pain and the coffee nerves.

She wasn't gone long, but having nothing but his own discomfort to think about made it seem long. When she came back he looked up at her expectantly, not really caring what her message was just so she'd distract him from himself, and she said, "You're to come with me."

Good. That was very distracting. "Where?" he said.

"Outside."

"Why don't I meet him in the hotel?"

"It was thought you would want privacy."

"You mean," Grofield said, "you people want privacy."

She shrugged. "Do you want to meet Mr. Marba or not?"

"All right. I'll come along." He got to his feet. "But no rough stuff, all right?"

She frowned at him. "I don't understand."

"I don't want to be beaten up, or drugged, or kidnapped, or anything like that. Okay?"

"Who would do anything like that?"

"You'd be surprised," he said. "Lead on."

She led, and the two of them crossed the lobby together, and Grofield had an actor's awareness of the picture they were making, the handsome actorish white man and the beautiful dramatic black woman crossing the baroque old Chateau Frontenac lobby together. Conversations and footsteps faltered all around them as they walked across the carpet and out the main doors.

The Chateau Frontenac has its own courtyard, where cars and cabs pull in. The main city is out to the right, and that's the way she went, Grofield going along beside her, down to the right and through the arch and out to the Place d'Armes, the main square of the old city. Because it was off-season, only one hansom cab was waiting there, the horse wearing a blanket and exhaling double plumes of steam, the driver bundled up in an old brown overcoat with a brown fur collar and a green and orange wool cap pulled down over his ears.

The girl said, "We'll take the cab. Tell him we want to see the Plains of Abraham."

Grofield hesitated. It was one thing to want to force the issue, it was another to go skipping away blindly into potential deathtraps. "I'm not sure about this," he said.

She gave him an impatient look. "What's the matter? No one's going to hurt you."

"I'm not so sure."

"I thought you said you knew Mr. Marba," she said.

Grofield considered her, and she was right. It was Marba's character he was relying on, and Marba's character seemed to him to be cold and calculating and detached, but not violent. He wouldn't consider approaching General Pozos like this at all, for instance, because of his idea of the general's character. If his idea of Marba's character was right, this approach was a sensible one and it didn't matter where they met. If his idea of Marba's character was wrong, this approach was doomed and it still didn't matter where they met.

He shrugged and said, "Okay. We'll do it your way."

They crossed the street and woke the hansom driver out of a half snooze. Grofield said they wanted to see the Plains of Abraham, and the driver nodded vigorously and blew his nose vigorously and began clucking vigorously at his horse, which was also more asleep than awake. Neither man nor horse seemed at all struck by their passengers' bi-racial nature.

Grofield and the girl sat side by side in the open cab. There was a heavy fur blanket on the seat across from them, and Grofield put it over both their laps. She thanked him, her first human touch, and the horse began to walk slowly forward, jerking the cab along behind him.

They traveled slowly around the Place d'Armes, a surprisingly dark square at night to be the middle of such a tourist area, and turned left up Rue Sainte Anne.

At first Grofield had no idea who was talking. A deep-throated muffled mutter seemed to hang in the air all around them, as though the fur blanket on their laps had decided to chat with them. But it wasn't the fur, it was the cabman, who from within the depths of his overcoat and a thick scarf and the wool cap was reeling off his usual tourist patter as the horse unhappily plodded along like any milkman's nag on the boringly familiar route. As they started up Rue Sainte Anne he told them they were passing the Anglican cathedral on their left, dedicated in 1804, the first cathedral of the Church of England ever built outside Great Britain. He gave more statistics, then went on to talk about the Price building and the Commercial Academy building and other ingots of fascinating lore.

Grofield looked at the girl, and found her grinning at him. She whispered, "Pay close attention, he gives an exam at the end of the trip."

He whispered back, "I can't decide if it's the man talking or the horse."

"It seems like the man," she whispered, "but it isn't. The horse is a ventriloquist."

Grofield looked at her in amazement. A complete transformation had taken place. She was suddenly pleasant, cheerful, absolutely friendly.

He supposed it was the open air, the riding together in this touristy conveyance, the shared notion that the statistically mumbling driver was funny. But the change was so radical he was having trouble believing it. He nearly made a comment on it, but held back, afraid that to point at the new personality might shatter it. He was in no hurry to see Miss Hyde again.

They found more things to talk about, whispering together under the murmur of the driver, talking about the horse and driver, the things he was saying, the signs and buildings they passed. Nothing other than that, nothing about the situation they were in, or the world around them, or themselves, or the hotel, or anything at all that wasn't prompted by specific things from the here and now. It was a slightly nervous feeling, skating along so totally on the surface like that, but she maintained it very well and he was always at his best when he had another good actor to work with, so while the horse clop-thumped pessimistically up Rue Sainte Anne, Grofield found himself ad-libbing a scene that might have been titled *The Blind Date That Worked Out.*

Meantime, they had turned left on Rue Dauphine. On their left, the driver grumbled at them, stood the Quebec Literary and Historical Society, in a building that was originally the Quebec jail. Public executions were once held in the courtyard behind the building, and in the basement tourists who got their kicks that way could still see the old cells.

A little past that they left the walled city, their driver informing them through his scarf that they were going through Kent Gate, built in 1879 by Queen Victoria in memory of her father. And after that, at last, he was quiet for a while.

This seemed to be a residential section, just beyond the wall, and even darker than the streets inside. Grofield began to get nervous again, and forgot about maintaining his part of the improvisation, which as a result faltered, and they rode in silence a little while, till they passed the Parliament, all lit up by flood-lights on the lawn. In the reflected glow, Grofield saw the girl studying him, and when he looked at her she laughed and said, "You really *are* afraid."

"Laugh at me later," Grofield said. "When nothing has happened."

"I will."

Ahead was Grande Allée, a major street, well-illuminated and with a traffic light, which was going to be against them. The girl leaned close and whispered to Grofield, "We are going to see a friend and be happy to see him and invite him to ride with us. You tell the driver it's all right."

Grofield nodded.

The intersection was getting close, and the light was still red. The driver grumbled at his horse, which immediately stopped.

The girl suddenly cried, "Ronald!" and half stood and waved an arm. "Look, dear," she said loudly to Grofield. "It's Ronald."

Grofield looked, and a man was coming this way across the sidewalk. He was tall and slender, but the light was behind him and Grofield couldn't see his face.

The girl was saying things about isn't-this-lucky, making a lot of happy noises. Grofield kept silent and watched, and when the man reached the side of the cab it was Onum Marba, on his face the small secret smile Grofield remembered from their last encounter, a year ago down in Puerto Rico. "How nice to see you both," he said, the tone straight but his expression ironic.

"You must come with us," the girl said. "We're going to see the Plains of Abraham." She jabbed a bony fist into Grofield's side.

"Uh," Grofield said. "Yeah, that's right. Come on, Ronald, come for a ride with us."

"If you're sure it's all right . . ."

"Of course it's all right," Grofield said. "Come on, the light's green."

"Thank you very much," Marba said. "I'd be delighted."

He climbed up into the cab, settling in the seat facing Grofield and the girl, the driver up behind his head. The driver had been half twisted in the seat, watching without much interest, and now Grofield said to him, "Okay, we're set."

The driver grunted, and faced front. He mumbled at his horse, and the animal plodded slowly across Grande Allée and entered the park called the Plains of Abraham.

Marba leaned forward, his face now indistinct again in the general darkness. His skin was not as dark as the girl's, it was more brown, but at the moment the effect was the same. He said, "You turn up in odd places, Mr. Grofield."

"We both do, Mr. Marba."

"I'm vacationing here," Marba said. "Are you vacationing?"

"Not exactly. I was shanghaied by some American espionage organization—not the CIA, some other outfit, they won't tell me what—and they sent me here to spy on you."

Marba showed humorous surprise, being surprised because it was expected of him but not working very hard to make Grofield believe it. "Spy on me? Why on earth would anyone from the United States government want you to spy on me?"

"Because we used to know each other. The idea being I should work my way into your confidence, find out what's going on, and then report."

"I hope they aren't wasting too much money on you," Marba said. "I am only here on vacation."

"Colonel Rahgos too?"

Marba smiled and said, "My President is not in Quebec."

"Not under his own name," Grofield said. "Neither are you. Neither is General Pozos. There are head men here from seven countries, three in Africa, two in South America, one in Central America and one in Asia, and they're all here under phony names. There may be people here from other countries, too. The kind of country these espionage people call the Third World."

Marba seemed to consider. Up front, the driver was mumbling away again about the historic battle between Wolfe and Montcalm, and it was beneath his patter that Grofield and Marba were having their conversation. Marba thought things over for half a minute or so, while the driver reported that both Wolfe and Montcalm were killed in the battle, and then he leaned close to Grofield again and said, "Setting aside for just a moment the ridiculousness of your implications—why would my President hold secret negotiations with leaders from South America, for instance?—but setting that aside, and taking it for granted you are telling me the truth insofar as you know it, why are you betraying your own people?"

"I'm not betraying anybody," Grofield said. "I was forced into this, it was come here or go to jail, and to tell you the truth I might have gone along with it and done what they wanted, if I could. But this afternoon I was kidnapped and drugged, and when I got back to my hotel room there was a murdered man in it, and the time has come for me to look out for Number One. My own people, as you call them, won't tell me anything, and the only other people I know around here are you and General Pozos. Of the two, you were likelier to be sober. And sensible. So I came to you."

"For assistance?"

"For information and advice. And assistance too, if I need it."

Marba smiled in amused admiration. "I remember the last time I saw you in action," he said, "how impressed I was by your ability to use truth as a weapon. You wouldn't be doing the same thing again, would you?"

"All I'm trying to do is get myself off the hook," Grofield said. "Same as last time."

"You do tend to get yourself in trouble, don't you? But I don't understand why you're being so open and truthful with me. Why not do what you were ordered to do, come to me as though innocent and see what you can learn?"

Grofield shrugged. "I know you," he said. "I wouldn't want to try to con you."

Marba smiled again, and waggled a finger in gentle reproof. "Grofield, Grofield, you're trying to con me now."

"How? I'm telling you the truth."

"It wouldn't be, would it, that you came to me because you knew I already *knew* the truth?"

Grofield sat back, studying Marba's face. "I must have a bad reputation with you," he said.

"On the contrary, my opinion of your abilities is very high."

"Would it do any good to say I didn't know you were onto me?"

"None. You can read signs as well as anyone. When Vivian didn't return to question you again, when I showed no further interest in you, it had to mean I'd investigated in other ways and learned enough to know what you were up to."

"You're right," Grofield said. "I should have realized that's what it meant. I guess I was too busy with everything else that was going on."

Marba smiled and shook his head. "It won't do, Grofield," he said. "Drop the denial, it will only cause bad feeling between us."

Grofield shrugged. "Consider it dropped."

"Good," said Marba. "Now tell me what you really want."

"Sure. I want two things. First of all, did you people kill Carlson?"

The girl made a sharp sound, and when Grofield turned his head to look at her she was staring at him in amazement. "That's a goddamn thing to say!"

"A little softer, dear," Marba said gently.

She looked quickly at him, then up at the driver's back. "I'm sorry," she said, much more softly, "but the arrogance of this man . . ."

"From his point of view," Marba told her, "it is a sensible question, and one he must ask." He looked at Grofield. "No, we did not. Murder has no part in our plans here this weekend. Nor has espionage, if we can possibly avoid it."

"You're bugging my room, aren't you?"

Marba smiled again. "A shot in the dark? Yes, you're perfectly right, we have a microphone in your room."

"Then you know who did kill him."

"We have his voice, of course. But not his name, or his face. Would you like to hear the tape?"

"I'd love it," Grofield said.

"When we get back, I'll arrange it."

The girl said something fast and low, in a liquid language Grofield had never heard before, but Marba answered her in English, saying, "Mr. Grofield isn't a threat to us, dear. And of course he knows we have him under surveillance. There's really no problem about playing that tape for him."

Grofield said to her, "And it's rude not to talk in English when I'm around."

The successful blind date had been packed away in a trunk again, and the girl who was sitting beside him now was once more cold and aloof and disdainful, coming on just as she had back in the hotel lobby. And in his room earlier today. She said, "It's rude of you to be in our company without learning our native tongue."

"Children," said Marba soothingly, the word and the manner oddly inaccurate from such a thin, controlled man. "We really don't have time for spats. Mr. Grofield, you said you wanted two things. The murderer of your friend was the first. What is the second?"

Grofield considered correcting the notion that Henry Carlson had been his friend, and then decided to let it go. He said, "I need a story. I personally don't care what you people are up to, I really don't believe it can be anything of life and death importance to the United States, but I'm going to have to give these espionage people a believable story before they'll let me go away and mind my own business again."

"You want me to give you a story to tell?"

"I'd like the two of us to work on it together," Grofield said. "You know what sort of thing you people *could* be here for, you know the sort of high-level political stuff that would sound right."

"What is my motivation for helping you?" Marba asked him.

"If I fail," Grofield told him, "the people who aimed me at you won't let it go at that. They'll try bugging your rooms, following you around, taking movies through keyholes, bribing waiters, all that sort of thing. They'll be a constant source of irritation all weekend even if they *don't* learn anything. But if you and I cook up a good believable story now, one they'll swallow and one that will soothe them about your purpose here, they'll go away and leave you alone and you'll have the weekend to yourselves."

Marba laughed, loudly enough to make the driver falter in his oral guidebook. The driver cleared his throat and went on, picking up his sentence again where he'd left off, and Marba said, "Grofield, I admire you, I truly do. You always find the most compelling reasons for everyone else to do the things that will benefit you."

"What's good for me is good for you," Grofield said. "I'm just lucky."

"Very lucky. All right, let me talk things over with some others, and I'll contact you again later on. I have no doubt your reasoning will win the day."

"Good."

Marba turned to the girl. "Vivian, when you return to the hotel, take Mr. Grofield up to the monitor room. I'll have called them by the time you get there to let them know you're coming."

Frowning, she said, "Is it good to let him see. . . ?"

"It's perfectly safe," Marba assured her. "Mr. Grofield won't do anything to endanger our alliance."

The girl shrugged irritably. She didn't seem entirely convinced, and she sat there with her arms folded and a stubborn look around her mouth.

The cab was just turning into Rue St. Louis, heading down the long one-way street at the far end of which was the hotel. Marba stood up and said, "I'll get in touch with you later, Grofield."

"I'll be waiting."

Marba nodded, and stepped down lightly from the cab while it was moving. Grofield waved to him, and then the cab went on, the horse clop-clopping on the stones, and Marba was out of sight. Three cars passed in the next minute, and he wondered idly which one of them contained Marba.

The girl hadn't changed her posture or the look on her face. She was staring straight ahead, angry and disapproving. Grofield, trying to pick up the blind date improvisation again, leaned toward her and said, "That motel on the right was built by the Algonquin Indians in 1746, in honor of the Blessed Virgin of Guadaloupe. In the basement there's the finest collection in North America of the eyeballs of martyred missionaries."

There was no response. She continued to glower, with folded arms.

Grofield said, "What's the matter? Don't you believe me?"

She gave him an ice-cold look. "I don't like you," she said, and faced front again.

Grofield said, "How come? On the way up everything was very pleasant."

She faced him again, still frozen-eyed. "If you must know," she said, "on the way up I thought you were a patriot. I thought you were working for your country out of conviction. A patriot might be my enemy, if his country was my country's enemy, but at least I would be able to respect him. But you aren't a patriot, you were forced to be here and you don't care at all that you are betraying your country. You don't care for anything but yourself, you don't understand the existence of anything larger than yourself. I despise you, Mr. Grofield, and I do not want to talk to you any more. And I don't want you to talk to me." She faced front again.

"Some day, Miss Kamdela," Grofield said, "we'll have a nice long talk about patriotism versus the draft. In the meantime, I'm going to take care of my own skin whether you approve or not."

Throughout the remainder of the ride back to the Place d'Armes and the hotel, he had plenty of silent time to consider the inadequacy of that response.

🍀

TWELVE

🍀

THE MONITOR ROOM WAS an ordinary hotel room on the Chateau Frontenac's fifth floor, rear view, full of open suitcases packed with electronic equipment. Five men were in the room, in rolled-up shirtsleeves, and it didn't take much conversation for Grofield to discover they were from the United States, electronics eaves-dropping specialists, private detectives hired for the occasion. Grofield grinned at Vivian Kamdela and said quietly, "More patriots from south of the border."

"One hires technicians," she said coldly. "One doesn't have to like one's employees."

"What a prig you are," Grofield told her.

The technician he'd been talking to called him now from across the room. He went over, followed by the girl, and the technician was threading a tape onto a small Japanese tape recorder. "Noise activates the tape," he explained. "If there's nothing happening, the tape doesn't run. So there might have been silent spaces in between the sounds you hear, but they won't show up on the tape."

"I understand."

"Just let me find the right place on the tape." He started the machine at *Fast Forward,* and for a few seconds the three of them stood there watching the reels spin around. Then he stopped it, switched to *Play,* and Grofield heard himself say, "Us counterspies work funny hours."

"It's later than that," the technician said, unembarrassed at Grofield standing there listening to himself being eavesdropped on, and switched to *Fast Forward* again.

Grofield said, "That was me talking to Carlson. When I woke up this afternoon."

"That's right," the technician said, and switched back to *Play.* This time it was Carlson's voice, saying, "You don't gain anything . . ."

"Too far." The technician switched to *Rewind,* then back to *Play.*

Grofield heard himself say, "But be sure the door is locked when you go out."

Carlson's voice said, "Certainly." The clarity was good, a little echo, the reproduction somewhat better than that of a telephone.

"Not that it does any good," Grofield's voice mumbled, and a door opened and closed.

There was a click, and the technician said in a quick whisper, "That's a jump in time."

Grofield nodded, listening to Carlson's voice again. "Henry here." A click. "He seems clean. The Kamdela woman was sent by Marba, to find out what he was doing here." A click. "Of course he's suspicious, everybody's suspicious. But he won't link Grofield with us if we're careful." A click. "I imagine he's trying to run out on us now. You know he knows about the transmitters." A click. "All right. I'll keep an eye on things at this end. I'll be upstairs if you need me." A click. "Right."

There was another click after that, and then a series of vaguer noises, movement, scuffing, small metallic sounds. Grofield gave the technician a puzzled look, and the technician said, "We've listened to this part a few times, and we think it's somebody working on the hall door. Was the door jimmied?"

"No."

"That's it, then. He's picking the lock. Listen, now."

Grofield listened. Softly, a door closed.

The technician said, "That's Carlson, going into either the bathroom or the closet, we don't know which."

"Too bad you didn't have television," Grofield said sarcastically.

The technician took it straight. "They didn't give us that kind of budget," he said. "Listen. Here's where the intruder comes in. Hear that?"

"Yes. What's that? He's opening drawers?"

"Yes. He gives the room a pretty good search. As a matter of fact, we were worried for a while he'd find our equipment."

"But he didn't."

"No. We did a good job stashing it."

"Where'd you put it?" Grofield asked innocently.

The technician grinned at him. "Sure," he said.

Vivian Kamdela said coldly, "He thinks he's clever."

The technician looked at her in surprise, and Grofield explained, "Just a lover's spat."

The technician grinned again, then harked back at his tape, saying, "Any second now."

The small sounds, like the burrowing of a pack rat in its lair, continued a few seconds longer, and then a door opened and there was a gasp, and a new voice, in heavily accented English, said, "Who are you?"

"I am Mr. Grofield," Henry Carlson said indignantly. "And this is my room. What are you doing here?"

"You are not Grofield," the other one said. "You better answer straight. Who are you?"

"You want to be careful with that," Henry Carlson said. "If it goes off, we'll have the whole hotel around our ears."

"I don't need this," said the other one. "I've got this."

"That must be the knife," the technician whispered.

Grofield nodded impatiently, having already understood that. Carlson, on the tape, was saying, "So I see. Well, there's no need to threaten me, you know. You don't gain anything that way. We're both interlopers, because you're not Grofield either."

The other one said suspiciously, "What have you got there?"

"My book," Carlson said. "I took it in with me. Just habit. You see, there's nothing inside it. Aya! For God's sake . . ."

The other voice, having broken into some foreign language, was apparently cursing. There were scuffling, bumping sounds, and Carlson said, "You . . ." in an explanatory way. Then Carlson coughed, and there were more thumping sounds. Then a click, followed by Vivian Kamdela's voice saying, "Carlson is dead. The other one isn't here. There doesn't seem . . ."

The technician switched off the tape. "What we think happened," he said, "Carlson had his book in his hand, with his finger marking the place. He was going to hold it up and open it so the other guy could see there wasn't anything inside, but the other guy got scared by the movement and lunged forward with the knife. Carlson stuck the book up like a shield and the knife went into it. It apparently went through enough to cut him the first time, but not badly, and with the book stuck all the way onto the knife the other guy stabbed him again, this time getting in a good shot."

"A wonderful shot," Grofield said. "Do you have any idea what language that was?"

"Sorry. We've listened to it, but nobody here knows it at all."

Grofield turned to Vivian. "You don't know it either?"

"If I did, I would say so."

"All right." Grofield looked back at the technician. "Could I have a copy of the tape?"

"You've got to be kidding," the technician said.

"Just the part with the foreign language on it."

The technician shook his head. "Not a chance of it."

"Why not?"

"Is that a real question?"

"Of course."

The technician glanced at Vivian, then looked back at Grofield. "What we have here," he said, patting the tape machine, "is evidence in a murder case. We are suppressing that evidence, because it's also evidence of illegal bugging and a few other breaking of laws that *we've* done. If we give you a copy of any part of this tape, you'll have evidence that we're suppressing evidence. Nobody likes you that much."

"I wanted to see if I could get that language identified. I wouldn't turn the tape over to the law."

"The kind of life you seem to live," the technician said, "you wouldn't have to turn it over to anybody. All you'd have to do was carry it around for a while, and sooner or later everybody would be in trouble."

Grofield looked suspiciously at Vivian. "Have you been talking about me behind my back?"

She gave a shrug of contempt and walked away.

The technician gestured at the tape machine. "That's what's been talking," he said. "You'd be surprised how much we've picked up since you moved into that room."

"No I wouldn't. Nothing surprises me any more."

"This isn't your regular line, is it?"

"How'd you know?"

"You better go back to your own field," the technician said. "Whatever it is, it's got to be safer than this."

"It is," Grofield said. "Thank you for letting me listen to that."

"Any time."

Grofield looked around, and Vivian was over by the door. He walked over to her and said, "I'm done here."

"Good," she said, and looked away from him.

Grofield said, "Don't you escort me any more?"

"You know where your room is."

"What about Marba?"

"He told you he would be in touch with you."

"I guess he did, at that. Have you had dinner?"

"Yes."

"Oh. Interested in having a drink?"

She gave him a cold look. "I am not going anywhere with you," she said. "Good-bye."

"I don't know why I try to be friendly with you," he said.

"I do," she said, and turned away, and walked off.

Grofield looked after her, and then called, "One of these times, I get the exit line."

She didn't bother to respond.

THIRTEEN

KEN WAS IN GROFIELD'S ROOM, but Henry was gone. Grofield walked in, shut the door behind him, and said, "Don't you have a place of your own?"

"I don't like you, Grofield," Ken said.

"Then go away." Grofield yawned and stretched, saying through the yawn, "You know, it's amazing. I've only been out of bed seven hours, and I'm exhausted again."

"It probably wore you out, worrying about your fellow man."

Grofield looked at him. "I know a girl you'd get along with great guns," he said. "Why doesn't it ever occur to you people that I'm *your* fellow man?"

"I'm not going to try to make sense out of that," Ken said. "Did you make contact?"

Acutely aware of all the listening ears, Grofield said, "Well, these things take time."

"We don't have time. They're only going to be here for the weekend. Haven't you contacted anybody at all?"

"One thing I've noticed about counterspy work," Grofield said. "Nobody asks questions unless they already know the answer. Meaning one of your people undoubtedly watched me meet Miss Kamdela in the lobby, and go for a ride with her."

"We know you met her," Ken said drily. "We don't know if it was business or not."

"If you knew Miss Kamdela," Grofield told him, "the question wouldn't come up. She's like you, she has no use for people who worry about themselves."

"I take it you mean it was a business meeting. What was the result?"

"I am to be contacted."

"By whom?"

"Onum Marba."

"You haven't met him yet, eh?"

Grofield waggled a finger at him. "There you go again, trying to be sneaky. If you ask the question, it means you know I've seen him."

"You're goddamn tiresome, Grofield."

"I was thinking the same about you, Ken. If you want straight answers, give me straight questions. Quit trying to be tricky."

"I know it's unfair of me," Ken said acidly, "but I just have this persistent feeling of mistrust where you're concerned."

"Fire me."

"At first, you know, you were kind of funny, I enjoyed the different point of view and so on. But you aren't funny at all any more, Grofield. I'll give you a straight question, if that's what you want, and let's see if you're capable of a straight answer. What did you and Marba talk about?"

"What was I doing here, and would there be any employment for me. See? When you're straight I'm straight."

"Maybe you are. What cover story did you give him?"

"I was in a robbery in the states that went *phloo*, and I'm hiding out in Canada till the heat's off."

"He knows that much about you? About the robberies?"

"Why not?" Grofield yawned again. "Listen," he said, "this is fun and all, but I'm really falling asleep."

"You don't have anything else to report?"

"Nothing."

"I have one thing," Ken said. "We checked into the background of Albert Beaudry."

"Who?"

"The kidnapper that was killed."

"Oh! The driver, up north. What about him?"

"He was a member of Le Quebecois."

"Sounds like a hockey team."

Ken looked at him. "I forgot about you," he said. "It's amazing the things you don't know. Are you aware at all of the Quebec separatist movement?"

"Not at all," Grofield said. "What's a Quebec separatist movement?"

"The province of Quebec," Ken told him, "is the one section of Canada that's more French than English. In language, customs, history, everything. For the last fifteen years or so, there's been an upsurge in the movement to get Quebec to secede from Canada and connect itself somehow politically with France. When De Gaulle was over here a few years ago he fanned the flames a little, and now there's half a dozen organizations devoted to an independent Quebec, ranging from the political through the vandal to the terrorist. Le Quebecois is the most radical of the groups, advocating armed rebellion, so naturally it's the smallest and least effective."

"Wait a second. Naturally? What do you mean naturally?"

"Where actual oppression doesn't exist," Ken said, "armed revolutionaries have a tough time gaining converts. A lot of youngsters don't mind smearing paint on the Wolfe side of the Wolfe-Montcalm Monument, but when it comes to taking a rifle and shooting people who speak English, most of them would rather not."

"I agree with them," Grofield said. "Wholeheartedly."

Ken gave a thin smile. "There are so many better reasons to shoot you, Grofield," he said, "it hardly matters what language you speak."

"I'm being good," Grofield reminded him. "Now you be good."

"I suppose you're right. Okay, Albert Beaudry belonged to Le Quebecois, the most radical and militant of the Quebec Libre groups."

"They *do* shoot people who speak English?"

"No, not generally. They advocate it, but if they actually did it they wouldn't last long."

"Then why'd they attack me? And why'd they speak English to each other?"

"They did?"

"In the car, on the way up to that cabin. I told you about that, I was conscious but I couldn't move."

"And they spoke English," Ken said musingly. "Was the other man also French-Canadian?"

"He had a different sort of accent," Grofield said. "Vaguely German, but not exactly."

"Dutch?"

"No, not really German at all. Just sort of harsh. German was the only thing I could think of that was like that at all."

"Hmmmm." Ken gazed into the middle distance, thinking about things. "That might explain it," he said.

"What might?"

"We couldn't understand," Ken told him, "what Le Quebecois was up to, we couldn't see any way they'd fit into this at all. But if they spoke English, Beaudry and the doctor, it would mean the doctor didn't speak French, so English was their only common language. So they might be Maoist somehow. There weren't any Chinese there, were there?"

"Chinese! Are you pulling my leg?"

"No I'm not. There's a thin thread of association from France to Red China, which I assume you didn't know."

"Go ahead and assume."

"The countries are very similar," Ken said. "France holds the same position as opposed to the United States in the Western bloc that China holds as opposed to Russia in the Eastern bloc. They're both big, stupid, well-armed nations being very shrill to cover their inferiority complexes. They're the two nuclear powers that are in some ways independent of the global balance of power, and their advocates in other parts of the world tend to be sympathetic to both nations. The Quebec Libre groups in Canada, for instance, have sympathetic ties to the Maoist groups in the black ghettos in the states."

In amazement Grofield said, "Am I the only one in the world who isn't involved in some crazy organization somewhere?"

"No, Grofield, you're one with the complacent majority. Most of these organizations have no more than ten or twenty people, and almost none of them have over a hundred. But they have more ultimate effect on the world than ten thousand people like you sitting in front of the television set letting Walter Cronkite make them informed and aware."

"There are worlds and worlds," Grofield said. "Mine has gotten along just fine for years without either you people *or* Walter Cronkite. All right, never mind the rebuttal. Are you trying to say this Albert Beaudry was being a spy for Communist China?"

"Possibly. Or possibly for France. Or possibly for some nation within the Chinese orbit, like Albania."

"Albania is within the Chinese orbit?"

Ken looked at him in astonishment. "You didn't even know *that?*"

"Good night, Ken," Grofield said.

FOURTEEN

A CHINAMAN WITH A RIFLE in his hands smiled cozily at Grofield and said, "Say something," but Grofield knew if he opened his mouth and said something in English the Chinaman would shoot him. But he didn't know any other languages, so he just stood there, helpless. "You must speak before the bell sounds," the Chinaman said, and almost immediately the bell sounded, and Grofield's panic woke him up. He sat up and grabbed frantically at the telephone to make the bell stop, but when he held the receiver to his ear he was afraid to speak because if he said something in English that rotten Chinaman would shoot him.

There was silence against his ear, and his mind was full of confusion and contradictions. Hotel room, hotel room. He was forgetting something.

A hesitant voice said, "Grofield?"

"Mm," he said, to make a sound, but not yet speaking in English. There was still too much confusion in his head, he didn't want to take the chance and turn out to have been wrong.

The voice said, "I'm sorry, did I wake you?"

"Mm."

"This is Marba. Would you prefer me to call back later?"

"Oh!" The name had done it, readjusting him to the waking dream, and now that the confusion was cleared from his head he also recognized the voice. "Hello, Marba," he said. "No, I'm all right now. What is it?"

"My superiors want to meet you. But not in the hotel, you can understand why."

"Sure." He shifted the phone to the other ear, got himself more comfortable against the headboard. "Do I get escorted someplace again?"

"Not exactly. Can you be ready to leave at ten o'clock?"

"What time is it now?"

"Twenty minutes before nine."

"Ten o'clock? Sure."

"Can someone come by your room now? To bring you something."

"That'll be okay."

"Good, then. I'll see you later."

"Right."

Grofield cradled the telephone and got shakily out of bed. The nervousness caused by the dream was still in him, making his movements a little shaky and uncertain, but as he moved around the room the reaction faded.

Despite his tiredness, it had been difficult for him to get to sleep last night, and after Ken left he'd wound up lying in bed, head propped on both pillows, watching *The Big Sleep* with dubbed-in French. Bogart would open that cynical sidewinder mouth of his and some portly nasal Frenchman's voice would issue forth. The girls were served better by the French substitution, which was in some ways an improvement on the original, the liquid language combining more naturally with the artificial come-on appearance than had the actresses' own flat, awkward delivery. Most of the commercial interruptions touted Canadian National Railways, also in French, and were nicely scenic. Loving shots of mountains and waterfalls are soporific anyway, and so is an endless dialogue in a language you don't understand, so by the end of *The Big Sleep* Grofield was ready for some sleep of his own, and he'd switched off the set, the lights and himself, until the Chinaman and the telephone had conspired to bring him shakily back to a world that might or might not be real.

He dressed quickly and was brushing his teeth when a knock sounded at the door. He walked across the room with the brush sticking out of his mouth to the right side and foam on his mouth like an imitation of rabies. He opened the door and a smiling bellboy was there with an envelope on a tray.

Grofield took the envelope, and while he rooted in his pockets for a quarter he tried to say thank you through a mouthful of toothpaste and toothbrush, but it didn't work. He found a quarter, which speaks louder than words anyway, put it on the tray, shut the door, and opened the envelope. Inside was a claim check, with a brief note: "The car will be waiting out front at ten." No signature, no heading.

Grofield put the claim check in his wallet and threw the envelope and note in the wastebasket. Then he went back to brush his teeth, but while he was rinsing he had second thoughts and went back to fish the note out of the wastebasket again. Eat it? A boy had to draw the line somewhere. Burn it? Somehow too melodramatic; he would feel foolish watching himself do it. So he carried it into the bathroom and flushed it away. The envelope happily had nothing on it but his name and room number, typed, so that could stay in the wastebasket.

He had breakfast in the hotel, seeing no familiar faces, and at ten o'clock went out the main door and gave the captain the claim check. "Just one moment, sir."

It was more like five, and then a green Dodge Polara was driven up by a scruffy man in blue work clothes who presented Grofield with a parking bill of two dollars. Grofield rooted in his wallet and came up with a pinkish Canadian two dollar bill—the Canadians not subscribing to the American notion of that denomination's bad luck qualities—which he turned over for the car keys. Then he got behind the wheel and drove through the arch and out of the courtyard.

He stopped in the first parking space he came to and looked around, but Marba was nowhere to be seen. Not Marba nor anyone else he recognized.

Now what?

He sat there a minute or so before it occurred to him to look in the glove compartment, and there he found a medium-sized manila envelope with a capital G written on it in ink. G for Grofield, no doubt. He opened the envelope and removed a roadmap of the city and a small piece of paper on which was typed, "Stop for the man in orange."

Oh, yeah? Grofield opened the roadmap and saw an ink line on it, meticulously marking his route from the Chateau Frontenac out of the city. It involved his driving through the old walled city, down to the harbor, and across Pont Sainte Anne on Route 54. The ink line then continued on Route 54 on up to the top of the map, where it ended in a little arrow pointing upward. So he was to take Route 54 out of town, that was all, and watch for a man in orange.

Quebec is one of those odd North American cities—New Orleans is another—in which a picturesque old section has been preserved in the middle of square miles of standard, dull city. Grofield now drove half a dozen blocks and was abruptly out of what he thought of as Quebec. From this point on he might just as well have been in Cleveland or Houston or Seattle. The anonymous *urbs* sprawled away on all sides, dressed in its undershirt.

The traffic was the standard fare, too. No longer was it a matter of nosing your car slowly through curving ancient streets, now there was the usual heavy flow of vaguely distracted housewives, making abrupt left turns and having to be honked at when the light turned green. Grofield drove among them, waiting them out, and by the time he'd reached the northern limit of his map most of the traffic was left behind.

This was the main road into the Laurentians, the mountain chain above the city, extending northward toward the Canadian woods. The road was four lanes for a while, leaving the city, but about ten miles north it narrowed to two.

It was a sunny morning, bright and cold, with clean snow packed thick on both sides of the road. Occasionally a city-bound truck, red or steel gray, the sun sparking from its windshield, passed Grofield, but mostly he was alone on the road now. Twice, cars full of men in hunting jackets tore by him, heading north for the moose, but he saw none coming back with their trophies tied to the fender.

He was about twenty miles north of the city when he saw a truck pulled off to the right of the road, facing the same way he was going. It was steel-sided and very dirty, with green canvas draped over the rear opening. Grofield paid little attention to it until he saw the man in the bright orange jacket step down from the cab and walk back toward the rear of the truck.

Was this the one? Or was it just a wary hunter, determined not to be mistaken for a moose? Grofield slowed down, and as he got closer the man in the orange jacket motioned to him to pull in behind the truck.

He did, and sat in the car with the motor running. The man in orange came over, and Grofield lowered the window. The man had a round face, a bushy mustache, and a Latin American accent: "Meester Marba ees in the truck."

"Where in the truck?"

"You suspicious? You wait."

He nodded, and walked heavily away to the rear of the truck and agitated the green cloth there. Grofield kept one hand on the gear lever, ready to leave if something went wrong.

Someone he didn't recognize stuck his head out through the green cloth, and he and the man in orange spoke briefly. The one in the truck glanced over at Grofield, nodded, and disappeared. A minute later Marba himself appeared there, and motioned to Grofield to come over.

"Okay," Grofield said, even though no one would be able to hear him. He switched off the engine and got out of the car. He walked over to the truck, and the man in orange said as he passed, "That's good. Suspicious, that's good."

"Thank you," Grofield said, and gave him a little bow, and went on to the truck.

Marba said, "Just a moment, we have a stepladder," and disappeared behind the green canvas again. A few seconds later a ladder was stuck through and leaned against the ground, and Grofield went up and through the opening in the canvas into the truck.

A light was on in the ceiling, but it wasn't very bright and the interior was full of people and things, causing multiple shadows. Still, it was bright enough for Grofield to see Marba's slightly sad, apologetic smile and the guns being pointed at him by two of the others.

Grofield showed his empty hands, and made no sudden movements. "What's the need for this?" he said.

"A small precaution," Marba said. "A minor inconvenience. Take your clothing off, please."

"Do what?"

"We have others here for you," Marba said, and motioned at a card table in the middle of the truck interior. A pile of clothing was laid out there, with socks and underwear on top.

Grofield looked around. Besides the two Latin American-looking guys holding guns on him, and their brother outside, there was an Oriental to his left, between him and the way out. Four others of various races were up toward the other end of the truck, uncrating machine guns.

Marba said softly, "You're more intelligent than that, Grofield. Don't even consider it."

"Why do you want my clothes?"

"It took us quite a while to understand what you meant when you told Carlson you were going to put your radio on. Not turn your radio on, *put* your radio on. And of course no radio went on, no sound of it."

"Oh," Grofield said. "That's right, you've been listening in, haven't you?"

"Quite profitably," Marba said. "We're in something of a hurry, by the way, so if you'd start changing while we talk I'd appreciate it."

"I don't have anything to say right now," Grofield told him, and reluctantly stripped and put on the new clothes. Everything fit except the shoes, which were too tight. "Those were my own shoes," he told Marba. "They weren't given to me by Carlson's people."

"We'd rather not take the chance," Marba said. "I'm sorry."

"These are too tight."

"Perhaps they'll stretch as you wear them."

"You aren't making me happy," Grofield said, and tied the shoes. In the meantime a bundle had been made of his old clothing and handed out through the green canvas to someone outside. Grofield said, "They'll go for a ride now, huh?"

"And so will we," Marba said. "This plank along the side here is, I'm sorry to say, the best I can offer you for seating arrangements."

"It'll be better than standing in these shoes."

"We tried to get your size. I am sorry."

"So am I," Grofield said, and sat down on the plank extending along the side of the truck. Marba sat down beside him and nodded to one of the men at the other end of the truck, who rapped a gun butt against the wall, and a few seconds later the truck jolted forward.

Grofield said, "I don't suppose there's any point asking where we're going."

"Why not? We're going north, up into the North Woods." Marba smiled thinly. "Don't look discouraged, Grofield," he said, "We aren't taking you away to murder you."

"What then?"

"It was decided the best thing to do with you was hold you until we finished our business here. On Monday you will be released."

"You're going to hold me for three days?"

"Yes."

"In the North Woods, in the middle of winter, with shoes that pinch my feet."

Marba smiled and patted Grofield's knee. "I knew your sense of humor would see you through," he said.

ᔕ

FIFTEEN

ᔕ

The truck stopped.

Grofield roused himself from a brown study. "We there?"

"No no," Marba said, smiling. "We have a long way to go yet. We're just stopping for lunch."

"Lunch?" Grofield looked at his wrist, but his watch wasn't there any more, it had gone away with his gabby clothing.

"Nearly one o'clock," Marba said. "Shall we go?"

The others had already started to get out of the truck, and Grofield and Marba joined them, stepping down into cold clear sunlight on a quiet street in what looked like a neat New England town. Grofield said, "Am I allowed to know where I am?"

"Certainly. This is Roberval, on Lake Saint John. We're about a hundred and seventy miles north of Quebec."

"I don't see the lake."

"I believe it's in that direction."

"What's north of here?"

"Very little. Woods, mountains, lakes."

"Roads?"

Marba smiled. "All in good time," he said, and took Grofield's arm. "We'll pay for lunch, of course."

The restaurant was a smallish white clapboard building, converted from a private home. Three bearded men in hunting jackets sat in a corner sharing a bottle of red wine and speaking together in French. There had been ten people in the truck, nine in the back and the driver, and they now spread themselves over three tables, generally segregating themselves by race. There were three Orientals, and they sat at one table. The driver was a Caucasian, possibly an American, and he sat with the two Latin Americans. That left Marba and two other blacks, who took the table beside the window overlooking the side street where the truck was parked. Grofield joined this latter trio, staying close to Marba.

The waitress spoke only French, but it turned out to be a language Marba knew, so there was no trouble. Grofield chose a veal cutlet and asked, "Does your expense account cover wine?"

"I believe so," Marba said, and ordered.

While waiting for their food, Grofield tried to start a conversation with the other two, but Marba said, "I'm sorry, they don't speak English."

Grofield looked at their stolid faces. They were both young and strong-looking, with burly shoulders and thick necks. Bodyguard types, who wouldn't be expected to communicate with words. "They speak French?"

"No. Nothing but a dialect you wouldn't have heard of."

Grofield looked at him. "Would I have heard it on that tape?"

"Tape?" Marba looked blank.

"The one your people played for me."

"Oh! Grofield, I've already assured you we didn't murder your friend Carlson."

"Have you listened to the tape?"

"Yes, of course."

"Did you recognize the language?"

"Toward the end, do you mean?"

"While he was killing Carlson, I mean."

Marba shook his head. "No, it wasn't familiar to me. But I don't believe it was an African language. It didn't seem to be related to any of the African languages I know."

Grofield looked around the room. "We've also got Asians," he said. "And Latin Americans. And God knows what else."

Marba smiled. "We could be termed heterogeneous," he said. "But I will tell you that we played that section of tape for different members of our party, and none of them recognized it. It doesn't appear to be an Oriental tongue, and it certainly isn't Spanish or Portuguese or any dialect derived from them, which would eliminate Latin America."

"You've eliminated the whole world," Grofield said.

"Not entirely. Ah, here comes our wine."

Grofield waited while the waitress poured wine into their glasses, and when she'd gone away again he said, "What part of the world is left?"

"A few corners," Marba said, and sipped at the wine, "Quite good," he said, and put the glass down. "Principally eastern Europe, of course," he said. "And here comes lunch."

SIXTEEN

Twenty minutes after they left Roberval the truck stopped again. Grofield looked up and said, "Lunch again?"

"We change vehicles now," Marba said. "Come along."

They all climbed down out of the truck again. Everyone but Marba and Grofield was heavily armed by now, with machine guns slung to their backs and automatics hanging from cartridge belts at their waists. Grofield felt as though he'd been caught up with the advance party of a guerrilla revolution. He said, "You people aren't here to take Quebec away from Canada, are you?"

Marba looked at him in surprise. "What an idea! Where do you think of such things?"

"How do I know? Maybe you're tied in with these Quebec Libre people. I'm a stranger here myself."

Marba smiled and patted his arm. "Don't fret yourself," he said. "Territorial expansion is not on our agenda this weekend. Come along."

Grofield saw now that there was a large frozen lake just past the truck, and on it a medium-size twin-engine plane fixed with skis for landing on ice. He went with the others as they tramped down through the snow and out over the ice toward the plane, all of them except the driver of the truck. When Grofield looked back, the truck was making a U-turn and going away.

He looked around, and there was nothing encouraging to be seen in any direction. Ahead lay the plane, with the blue-white expanse of frozen lake beyond it. On the other three sides the snowbound shore. A few structures were visible a distance away, but none of them looked inhabited.

How had he gotten himself into this? Up in the frozen north without his electric long johns, with Marba and his friends really putting him on ice for the duration. Even if he could slip away from this well-armed bunch, there was nowhere for him to go. And even if he had somewhere to go, there was nothing for him to report to Ken and *his* bunch. And he knew Ken disliked him enough by now to take any excuse to ship him back to face that robbery rap.

What if he tried to get away from Marba *and* Ken? There was always the chance that Marba and his people would let it go at that, but Ken wouldn't. An entire espionage outfit from the United States Government would turn its energies to finding one Alan Grofield, actor/heistman, and however inept they were in their dealings with the Third World it was Grofield's gloomy conviction they could hold their own against one Grofield.

Not that there was any point thinking about his options and trying to make plans. The fact was, he didn't have any options, and all his plans had already been made for him by other people. The only thing left for him to do was keep his eyes wide open and try somehow still to be alive on Monday.

The plane's engines were already turning over as they all clambered aboard. Grofield, totally adapted to the jet age, found it strange to see propellers whirling ahead of the wings, blowing snow into everybody's face as they boarded. He found himself mistrusting the plane, and visualizing an icy death on some remote snowy mountainside near the Arctic Circle.

The plane was only nominally a passenger job, with hinged bucket seats that could be let down along both sides, so the group sat in two facing rows. There was no heat, and the metal seat was cold even through the overcoat Grofield wore. He tucked his hands in his pockets, hunched his shoulders, and gloomily watched everybody breathing steam.

The plane took off almost at once, trundling forever along the ice, going very slowly, almost reluctantly, bumping and trembling and apparently trying to shake itself apart rather than fly, but finally lifting as though the task were more than it could bear. Never had a plane seemed so conscious of its own weight, and that remote snowy mountainside loomed once again in Grofield's mind.

But once they had climbed to their cruising altitude, the plane settled down and began to behave, sailing along smoothly and matter-of-factly through the sky. Grofield, twisting around to look down past his elbow and out the small side window, saw remote snowy mountainsides down there, and here and there the glint of sunlight reflecting off frozen water. Lakes and snow, and then dark greenery, the Canadian North Woods.

It was louder inside the plane than in a New York City subway car, but Grofield tried to talk anyway, shouting into Marba's ear, *"Do we fly long?"*

On the second try he heard Marba's response: *"Less than an hour!"* So that wasn't too bad.

He'd never realized before now just how used he was to carrying a watch. Now he felt lost without it, without being able to compartmentalize his day. He didn't know how long they'd been in the air, he didn't know when an hour would be up, how much longer he could expect them to travel, and the result was that everything seemed much slower. He was sure an hour had gone by, and still they droned on through the sky. He was sure an hour and a half had gone by. He was sure two hours had gone by.

He didn't want to ask Marba. He wasn't sure why, but it just didn't seem to him that he wanted to ask Marba what time it was, or how long had they been in the air, or how much longer now till they landed. It would in some way be a confession of weakness, and therefore it had to be avoided.

But he came very close to asking anyway, eventually reaching the point where he decided to count slowly to a hundred, and if the plane hadn't started to land by then he would ask. So he began counting, in his head, and he was at three hundred twenty-seven when the plane abruptly banked to the right, tilting Grofield's side of the plane down and making him jump, startled.

Everyone else jumped too, and then all grinned sheepishly at one another, the expressions strangely at variance with all the artillery they wore draped all over themselves. Grofield looked away from the contrast and out the window again, and way below there was another frozen lake, with what looked like rough wooden buildings clustered together beside it. And smoke coming from two or three chimneys.

The plane circled once, dropping gradually, sliding down an invisible spiral chute, and then came straight in toward the lake, now seeming to be going far too fast, the surrounding mountains rushing by, covered with snow and pine trees. They hit badly, joltingly, the plane creaking and groaning in protest, as though someone had tossed a fifty-pound sack of potatoes on a porch glider. Then they swerved a little, but the pilot got things under control again and they rolled with relative smoothness across the lake to an easy stop.

The silence seemed to be full of humming, when the engines switched off. Grofield yawned to pop his ears and the humming changed in tone but remained present. He said, "I don't think much of your air force."

Marba smiled. "We have to make do with what the major powers leave us," he said. He got to his feet, and Grofield got up with him.

There was no one outside the plane to greet them. It couldn't be later than three o'clock, but the sun was a red ball low in the clear sky, and lights shone in the buildings on shore. They looked warm and cozy and comfortable, and Grofield happily joined the others scrunching across the snow-covered ice toward them. He said to Marba, "What is this place?"

"Once a logging camp, I believe," Marba said. "More recently a private hunting lodge. At the moment, it has been loaned to us."

"By whom?"

"A sympathizer," Marba said, and offered his cool smile again.

"I like how you answer all my questions," Grofield said.

"Of course. I hide nothing from you."

The sound of engines made Grofield look back, and damn if the plane wasn't turning around. Grofield watched and it trundled away across the ice, apparently planning to get into position to take off into the wind. He said, "That's going away too?"

"It will return for us," Marba said, and took Grofield's elbow. "Let's get inside where it's warm."

SEVENTEEN

I̲T̲ W̲A̲S̲ A̲ L̲O̲N̲G̲ R̲U̲S̲T̲I̲C̲ R̲O̲O̲M̲ with a high cathedral ceiling and with blazing fireplaces at both ends. Moose heads and color panoramas of mountain lakes decorated the walls, and fur rugs were scattered here and there on the floor and furniture. Multiracial groups of men were clustered, standing and seated, around the two fireplaces, leaving the center of the room, into which Grofield and the others now came, unpopulated.

Some people turned their heads when the door opened and the new group came in, but then they returned to their hot drinks and quiet conversations. All except one short and very fat man in a maroon uniform with gold piping and many, many medals clinking together on the chest and a long sword hanging down from his left side, who came trundling over from the fireplace to the right, arms outstretched for a bear hug. "Grofield!" he shouted, in melodramatic Spanish-accented enthusiasm. "The man who saved my life!" A few others turned to watch, attracted by the shout, while the fat man rushed up and embraced Grofield, burying his face in Grofield's chest, wafting upward the aromas of food and brandy and perspiration.

"Hello, General," Grofield said, struggling to keep his balance. Apparently the General didn't remember that the only other time he and Grofield had been in each other's area they hadn't exactly become fast friends. That had been on the General's yacht, and the General had been spending his days in bed, recuperating from a bullet in the chest.

But if the General now wanted to believe that Grofield was a long-lost buddy, it was perfectly all right. No harm done. So Grofield said, "It's good to see you again, General. All recovered?"

"Of course!" the General cried, releasing Grofield and stepping back to pound himself on the chest. "Can a pig kill General Pozos? Nonsense!" He spied Marba then, beside Grofield, and shouted, "*You* know this man! Didn't I send him to you in Puerto Rico?"

"You certainly did," Marba said. "And he was a pleasure to watch."

The General lowered his head and stared meaningfully at Marba through his eyebrows. In a completely different tone he said, "We must talk."

"No doubt," Marba said drily.

"Your Colonel is a very stubborn man."

"I agree," Marba said. "But I don't believe we should discuss business in front of our friend Grofield."

"Don't mind me," Grofield said.

The General looked at Grofield. The happy reunion was over, and the General's eyes were cold and impatient. "You will go now," he said.

Marba said, "I'll have someone show you to your room." He turned to one of the black men who'd come in with them and spoke to him in what sounded like the same language he and Vivian Kamdela had used together in the hansom cab. The other man nodded, and gestured to Grofield to come with him.

"See you later, General," Grofield said.

The General nodded brusquely, impatient for Grofield to be gone.

Grofield followed the black man away from there. They crossed the room and went through a doorway into a library lined with books and warmed by another huge fireplace. A few people sat around reading books, and didn't glance up as Grofield and his guide passed through.

The library was followed by a hall, which was followed by a door to the outside world. Feet had worn a path in the snow, a long, parabolic curve to a neighboring low building. The entrance was at one end of the building, and the interior was a long hall lined with doors. It looked like a fifth-rate motel, with wall partitions of cheap plasterboard, a floor of black linoleum apparently laid directly on plywood, and a ceiling of blank wooden panels. A row of fluorescent lights gave illumination.

The doors even had numbers on them, starting with 123 on Grofield's left and 124 on his right. The numbers declined as he and the black man walked down the hall, and it was number 108 that the black man finally opened, gesturing to Grofield to go in. Grofield did, and the door was closed behind him. He turned around, surprised, and heard a padlock being snapped shut.

Oh, nice. After all he'd gone through to avoid prison, now look.

He heard receding footsteps, creaking and squeaking on the linoleum-and-plywood, and waited a full minute before trying the door. Then it opened, very slightly, and caught with a little *clink* sound. Grofield pushed experimentally, not very hard, and nodded to himself. It was a hasp lock, at about the height of his waist, held with a padlock. That sort of arrangement would be no better than the wood into which the screws had been driven to hold the hasp lock pieces on, and judging from the general tone of the construction around here that wood was unlikely to be too awfully good.

All right. He pulled the door shut again and turned around to look at his new home.

He didn't like it. The bed was narrow and hard-looking, with metal headboard and footboard, a thin pillow, and scratchy-looking, thin gray blankets. A small rag rug was on the floor beside the bed, the rest of the floor continuing the linoleum-over-plywood theme from the hall. There was a battered metal dresser opposite the bed. A wooden kitchen chair completed the furnishings.

To Grofield's right there was a curtained partition. He pushed the curtain to one side and looked at a toilet with an overhead water closet. There were a number of clothes hooks on both side walls, so apparently this cubicle doubled as a closet.

The outer side of the partition wall contained a sink, with a somewhat distorted small mirror hanging crooked above it. On the opposite wall was a window, with a view of snow, and under the window an electric radiant heat unit. Since the room was a bit chilly Grofield went over and checked the unit and its one dial was turned to *high*.

Well, this would never do. He went across the room again and kicked the door open. It took three kicks, one more than he'd expected. He walked back down the corridor to the exit, and followed the curving path again back to the main building, holding his overcoat lapels closed under his throat while in the open air. He retraced his steps through the hall and the library into the main room, looked around, and saw Marba and General Pozos and two other men sitting in a cluster in two facing sofas near the fireplace on the left. He walked over there and said, "I'm sorry, Marba, but I don't like that room."

They looked at him in astonishment, and Marba looked quickly around, but Grofield said, "Oh, he locked me in. But the locks are no good in a place like this, you ought to know that."

The General was glowering. The other two men, one Oriental and one black, were looking puzzled and annoyed. Marba got to his feet and said, "Are you out of your mind, Grofield? Do you want to force us to kill you?"

"Marba, face it. I'm not going to get away from here on my own. As far as I've seen, I'm the only Anglo-Saxon in the joint, so I ought to be easy to spot. Just leave me alone. I'll sit in front of the fire, read a book, play checkers with somebody. There's nothing I can do to help the United States Government, and there's nothing I can do to help myself, and I know that, and I'll be a very good guest."

Marba stood there frowning, considering things. Finally he shook his head and said, "You're too unorthodox, Grofield, that can't be good."

"Have you seen that room? Would you go in there without a radio, without a book, without even a watch, and not know how long you're expected to stay, and just sit on that bed in there and be a good boy and wait?"

"There are worse places to be," Marba said.

"We could put you outside," the General said, and pointed a finger at Grofield. "You know I don't like funny people," he said. "Don't be funny people, Grofield. Go back to the room."

"I don't want to."

"Damn," Marba said. "Gentlemen, I'll be right back. Come along, Grofield." He started quickly away, taking Grofield's arm, and Grofield felt the General's eyes on him as he went. Marba was saying, under his breath, "Don't antagonize General Pozos, you damn fool. He *will* put you outside."

"I'd just come back in."

Marba stopped and looked hard at Grofield. "Don't say what you'll do or what you won't do. You're a prisoner here, don't you know that?"

"As Oscar Wilde once said, 'If this is the way the Queen treats her prisoners, she doesn't deserve to have any.'"

"I like you, Grofield," Marba said. "You're a very interesting and a very amusing variant of human life. But you must understand that several of the men up here this weekend are used to being in supreme command, they come from nations they rule with a whim of iron. If you irritate them, they won't think twice about getting rid of you. And if it becomes dangerous for me to protect you I'll leave you completely on your own. So do try to restrain yourself."

"I'll try," Grofield agreed. "But I'm not going to be locked up in that Hoover village out there."

"I don't understand the reference," Marba said, then added,

"But never mind. Just come along. And let me do the talking."

"Fine by me."

Their route lay through the library again, and this time one or two of the readers frowned in puzzlement at Grofield as he went by. He was, as he'd said, the only Anglo-Saxon here, and very noticeable, and he did tend to keep going back and forth through this room. He didn't know what any of them might think of it exactly, but he reminded himself of the mechanical bear at the shooting gallery: hit it, and it turns around and travels the other way. Under the circumstances, not an encouraging image.

After the library, this time the course ran differently, up narrow stairs to a second-floor corridor and through a door into a small anteroom very full of a large black man who bore many similarities to Sonny Liston. Marba said something in his native language to Sonny, who looked without expression at Grofield and slowly nodded. He was standing there with his arms crossed over his chest, harem-guard style, and he was all biceps and a yard wide.

Marba said to Grofield, "Wait here."

"Anything he says," Grofield agreed, nodding at the guard.

Marba offered his thin smile, and went through the other door, in the opposite wall. Grofield considered idle conversation with Sonny and decided not to try it. Instead, he sat down on the brown leather sofa that took up all of the room not occupied by Sonny, and tried to make believe he was taking it easy.

Would it have been better to stay in that stinking room? Safer, maybe, but better? No, no matter what, it was better to be away from there, it would have done bad things to his personality, he would have emerged from that room on Monday a pessimistic old man with false teeth. Improperly fitted false teeth.

And there was something else to consider, and that was Ken. Would Ken believe that he'd been kidnapped? Would Ken believe anything other than that Grofield had tried to get away again and this time had managed to give his pursuers the slip? One way or another, Grofield was going to have to go back to Ken with some sort of demonstration of his own sincerity and willingness and hard work. The best thing would be information on what this weekend's get-together was all about, but failing that much of a plum there had to be *some* sort of earnest of his good intentions he could pick up here this weekend and give Ken as a peace offering on Monday. But he couldn't do it if he was wasting away in that God-Is-Love Shelter for Homeless Men back there.

Of course, if General Pozos and the other bigwigs decided to shove him outdoors to freeze to death the whole problem would become academic, and he would be very sorry indeed he hadn't stayed in his nice little room, but at the moment he had high hopes—or at least medium hopes—that he could work this bloodless rebellion and get away with it.

While thinking about this, and giving himself qualified encouragement, the inner door opened and Marba came back out, shutting the door behind himself. He looked worried, and that made Grofield worried.

Marba sat down beside Grofield on the sofa. Speaking softly, he said, "What did you do to Vivian Kamdela?"

"Me? Nothing."

"She dislikes you."

"I know."

"Why?" Marba asked him.

"Because I'm not a patriot," Grofield said. "We had a little discussion, and I'm not patriotic enough to suit her. I tend to worry about myself first, and she doesn't approve of that. Why?"

"She's in there talking against you," Marba said. "If I could get Colonel Rahgos to vouch for you, you would be given fairly free rein here."

"Colonel Rahgos. He's your president, isn't he?"

"Yes. Generally he'd go along with my recommendation, but Vivian is arguing against you, quite forcibly. So he wants to see you for yourself, and whatever you do, be polite. The Colonel doesn't like flippancy."

"I'll be good," Grofield promised.

"The idea is to get the Colonel to like you."

"Should I give him a lock of my hair?"

"No," Marba said flatly. "It's the wrong shape."

"Oh, wonderful," Grofield said, and Marba took him to his leader.

EIGHTEEN

IT WAS A RUSTIC DRAWING ROOM, with a sofa and several chairs in a semi-circle in front of a deep stone fireplace, in which logs crackled and burned. Vivian Kamdela sat on one of the chairs, legs crossed, arms folded, eyes glaring at Grofield. She looked beautiful and nasty.

Standing in the middle of the room, a glass in his hand, was a tall, thin black man with gray-white hair and horn-rimmed glasses. He wore a dark gray business suit and a narrow dark tie, like an insurance salesman, but ruby rings glinted on both hands. He looked shrewd, intelligent, calculating, impatient, and cold as ice.

Marba said something in his native tongue, Grofield recognizing his own name planted strangely in the middle of all the foreign syllables. Then he said to Grofield, "This is Colonel Rahgos."

"How do you do, sir?"

"I do well." There was a British accent in the cultured voice, with some other accent half hidden behind it. "Do you drink whiskey?"

"Yes, sir." Grofield put his overcoat over the back of a chair.

"This is African whiskey," the Colonel said, "our own native whiskey. If you would prefer Canadian . . ."

"I've never had African whiskey," Grofield said. "I'd like to try it."

The Colonel nodded at Vivian Kamdela. Without changing her affronted expression, she uncrossed her long legs, got to her feet, and walked over to the bar. She looked good in dark green ski pants and a brown turtleneck sweater.

The Colonel was talking. Grofield brought his attention back from the ski pants, and the Colonel was saying, "You have never traveled in Africa?"

"No, sir. I've never been out of the Western Hemisphere."

"You prefer home."

"I like to travel, but I do like to go home again, yes, sir."

"Everyone loves his native land."

"Not necessarily the whole land," Grofield said. "But I do love the part I know. My wife, my friends, my home."

"You are married?"

The green ski pants were coming back. "Yes, sir. My wife's name is Mary."

Vivian Kamdela handed him an old-fashioned glass. In it was a pale yellow liquid, a good three ounces of it, and no ice. In color, it looked mostly like flat beer. There was a glint in her eye as she handed him the glass that might have been savage amusement.

Grofield looked from the glass to the Colonel. "I usually take my whiskey with ice," he said.

"Our whiskey doesn't need ice," Vivian said. "Ice destroys the bouquet."

The Colonel didn't say anything. He just stood there and watched.

Grofield had a feeling he was in for trouble. He lifted the glass to his lips and took a cautious sip and acid cut a groove through his tongue and straight down his esophagus into his stomach.

There was no question of faking a reaction. His eyes were watering, and he had no usable vocal cords at the moment. He stood there blinking, holding the glass up beside his face, trying to swallow and not choke.

Was that amusement in the Colonel's eyes? Hoping it was, Grofield cleared his throat and tried to talk. Hoarsely he said, "Oh, I wouldn't want to spoil *that* bouquet. Oh no."

"Is our whiskey too strong for you?" The Colonel smiled. "Perhaps it's a weakness in the white race. Perhaps white men's throats are softer." He lifted his own glass, with about an ounce of the same yellow liquid in it, made an ironic toasting motion, and drank the whiskey down. His eyes didn't water, he didn't clear his throat. He extended his empty glass toward Vivian and said, "Again, please. And some ice for Mr. Grofield."

Her expression was undisguised satisfaction as she held her hand out for Grofield's glass. He started to hand it to her, then paused, looking at it, and said, "Is this glass also African?"

The Colonel frowned. "No, it was here."

"Oh," Grofield said, and handed the glass to Vivian, who frowned at it for a second in puzzlement before turning to go back to the bar.

The Colonel said, "I don't understand the question about the glass."

"I was just wondering if it was also one of your national products. I'm sorry I really don't know very much about your country, Colonel, but for that matter I don't know very much about my own country."

"I understand you were forced into becoming a spy, it was not the result of patriotic conviction."

"Being a spy," Grofield said, "is very grubby work. It's like being a process server. I don't see how anybody could do it for noble reasons."

"Not to aid one's country?"

"If a man has nothing better to offer his country," Grofield said, "than his ability to listen at keyholes, he isn't much of a man."

"What do you offer your country, Mr. Grofield?"

"Apathetic allegiance. I'm not what we call a gung-ho type."

"I don't know the phrase, I'm sorry."

"It means I haven't devoted my life to serving my country." Vivian had come back with the drinks, and Grofield took his and said, "I'm like most people. The Canadian who made this glass didn't make it for Canada, he made it for a dollar an hour. Does that make him unpatriotic? And did the people who made the whiskey really do it for the greater glory of Undurwa?"

"Why not?" the Colonel said. "Why shouldn't every man do his very best, at whatever his trade, for the sake of his homeland?"

"You mean the individual makes himself secondary to the state. I'm not very up on politics, but I believe my country is on the other side of that argument."

"In theory," the Colonel said. "Tell me, have you ever seen Harlem?"

"I was wondering when that would show up," Grofield said. "Colonel, I've never seen Harlem and I've never seen Palm Beach and I think we can pretty well establish I'm not St. Francis of Assisi, but then who is? If I was a selfless greater-glory guy I'd be doling out soup at a Salvation Army mission right now and I wouldn't have gotten myself into the mess that had me dragooned up here. I know what my sins are, and I assure you politics isn't one of them."

The Colonel's eyes glinted in amusement. "Politics is a sin?"

"You were the one who brought up Harlem."

The amusement faded from the Colonel's eyes. "That's one way to look at things, of course. But I think we should get to the issue at hand. Is your drink better that way?"

"I haven't tried it yet," Grofield said, and tried it, and it was better. It was still white lightning, but drinkable. The explosion now didn't take place until the whiskey was all the way down in his stomach. "Much better," he said. "Thank you."

"The question seems to be," the Colonel said, "whether to kill you or let you live. You have insisted you won't be imprisoned, which would be the humane compromise, so we must select one or the other of the extremes. Is that a fair description of the situation?"

"Unfortunately, yes," Grofield said.

The Colonel nodded and turned away, pacing a few thoughtful steps, then stopping with his back to Grofield to gaze at the window—outside, night had fallen in mid-afternoon—and then to take a sip of his drink. Finally he looked back at Grofield and said, "You understand, of course, it is a human failing, when one is pushed one tends to push back."

"I don't mean to push anybody," Grofield said.

"You refuse to be imprisoned, *that* is a form of push." The Colonel abruptly smiled and said, "That's interesting, isn't it? You can refuse to be imprisoned, but you can't refuse to be killed. An odd situation, don't you think?"

Grofield's answering smile was rueful. "Very odd," he said.

"So you're a good American after all," The Colonel said. "Following in the footsteps of Patrick Henry. Give me liberty or give me death, am I right?"

"I guess you are."

"Yet when Mussolini said the same thing in different words," the Colonel said, "the American people thought him despicable."

"That sounds like politics again," Grofield said.

The Colonel studied him. "Are you truly apolitical, or is it a tactic?"

"Both."

The Colonel nodded slowly, thinking things over, and finally said, "Even if I were to give you your life, you wouldn't keep it. Sooner or later you would antagonize someone else here, and that would be the end of you. And then the question would be raised, who let this man wander around free like this? It would cause me embarrassment."

"I'll be very quiet," Grofield promised. "I won't cause any trouble at all."

The Colonel shook his head. "No. It's your nature to cause trouble. I was given two descriptions of you before you came here, so dissimilar I couldn't believe they were both describing the same man. That's partly why I wanted to see you for myself, and now I see that both descriptions were right, and you are potentially more trouble than either description alone could suggest. You have given me no compelling reason to want to keep you alive . . ."

"There's no compelling reason to kill me," Grofield said. "I'm not a danger to anybody."

"You *could* be. It's simpler to end the possibility before anything happens."

"That's an awfully small reason to end a human life."

"A human life is a very small thing."

Grofield said, "Is yours?"

The Colonel's smile was cold. "Mine is not at issue. Yours is. I see no reason to exert myself on your behalf."

Grofield looked at Marba, but Marba's face was closed and expressionless. He wasn't about to argue with his president on Grofield's behalf, and Grofield couldn't really blame him. He looked at Vivian, and her look flicked away, she wouldn't meet his eyes. Was that uncertainty in her face? It could be, but not enough to mean anything. Could he get her to change her mind at this point? Impossible.

Still, there was no point leaving any shot unfired. "Vivian," he said.

She got to her feet and turned her back, stood gazing into the fire.

The Colonel said, "It is not her decision, Mr. Grofield, it is mine. Neither she nor Mr. Marba could alter it."

Grofield looked at him. "And it's no?"

"I will send word," the Colonel said. "Marba will now take you back . . ."

It was no. A yes would be given to him right here and now, there wouldn't be any reason not to. But a no was more safely and neatly delivered by messenger.

Grofield looked at Marba again, and saw faintly that Marba was sorry it had worked out this way. Sorry, but passive.

The Colonel was saying, "It was an interesting experience, meeting you, Mr. Grofield. My personal contact with Americans has been more or less limited to diplomatic personnel, an entirely different breed from your . . ."

Grofield threw his drink in the Colonel's face, hit Marba on the side of the jaw, threw the glass at Vivian Kamdela's head, hit the Colonel in the pit of the stomach, grabbed up his overcoat from the back of a chair, and jumped through the window.

※

NINETEEN

※

THE OVERCOAT WAS DRAPED over his head to protect his face from flying window glass, his body was rolled up in a ball to protect himself from unknown dangers, and he was falling through the air, on his way from the second-story window toward who knew what.

He landed in snow, thunking into it like a fist in bread dough, and kneed himself in the chest, knocking the wind out of himself. He lay all wrapped up in the overcoat for a few seconds, the material against his forehead, the whiskey warmth of his breath soft on his cheek, and gradually got himself together again. Then he kicked his way out of the overcoat, like a butterfly emerging from its cocoon, stood up in powdery snow into which he was sinking nearly to the knees, and looked up at the broken window from which he'd emerged.

Vivian Kamdela was up there, silhouetted by the light in the empty frame. Savagely he wished he had a gun right now, but then he saw that she was making shooing motions. She glanced over her shoulder, into the room, then leant frantically out the window, shooing him away.

"Women," he grumbled. Changeable was one thing, but this was goddamn ridiculous. He picked up his overcoat, shook the snow off it, shrugged into it, and went plowing away through the deep snow, lifting his knees high, looking like a football player on slow-motion replay.

He didn't know where he was going to, but he knew where he was going from; anything with lights. He headed into the darkness straight ahead, grateful there was no moon in the clear sky. Starlight reflecting from the snow made shapes visible from fairly close, but the darkness should be complete enough to hide him from any pursuit.

The only problem was running. Having to climb from step to step like this was exhausting, and within a dozen steps he was bushed. He kept going though, having no choice in the matter, but finally it was impossible to yank his legs through the snow any farther, and he turned around, tottering, to see no pursuit.

No pursuit? Why not?

Obviously pursuit had started, Vivian Kamdela had had no other reason for such frantic signaling to him. So what had happened to it?

Then he saw the deep furrow of his tracks in the snow, and understood. Wiser heads had prevailed in there. He could hear it now: "Why run around in the dark after him? He isn't going anywhere. All we'll have to do is follow his trail in the morning."

Right.

If he was still alive in the morning. It was colder than hell out here. While he'd been running his exertion had kept him warm, combined with the whiskey he'd drunk, but now that he was standing still he could feel just how cold it was out here. His cheeks and the backs of his hands already had that cracked-glaze feeling of intense cold, and his earlobes had started to ache.

There were gloves in his overcoat pockets and he put them on, knowing they really weren't thick enough, but they would help a little. For his head and ears he had nothing.

Nor for his feet. He was wearing ordinary socks and shoes, and they were soaking wet already, snow down inside both shoes, melting against his arches. It wouldn't take long to develop frostbite that way.

All right. The name of the exercise was Survive, and the first thing to do was get himself organized and figure out exactly where he was in relation to the lodge and its outbuildings.

Ahead of him, succulent with yellow-lit windows, was the main building, out of which he'd just jumped. This was the rear of the building, opposite the side where he'd first gone in, meaning the lake was around on the other side of the cluster of buildings.

To the left of the main lodge, lower and with fewer lit windows, was the motel-like structure he'd been in briefly, in his salad days. Another similar structure was to the right. Farther to the right was a bulky shape without the definition of lights in its windows, a dark squared-off building, two stories high but not as broad as the lodge.

That looked like the logical first stop. It was shelter, and the absence of light suggested it was at the moment unoccupied. Grofield headed in that direction, not rushing this time but just plodding steadily along through the snow, feeling the tingles in his feet and ears and face and fingertips. His ankles and wrists were very cold, and he vaguely remembered reading somewhere that one should keep one's wrists and ankles warm because that's where the blood is closest to the surface and you don't want to cool your blood. At the moment, however, there wasn't much he could do about it.

Flashlight. Grofield stopped, and saw the light bobbing out from the lodge. A second later, another one followed. Not coming directly this way, but traveling at an angle to Grofield, so that his route and their route would intersect—

—at the building Grofield was heading for.

The bastards. They'd thought it over and decided Grofield would go to ground in the empty building, and they didn't want that. It would be so much simpler and neater for everybody if Grofield would just quietly freeze to death overnight, out in the refreshing air. Then they could come out in the morning and see if he'd checked out in an interesting position—standing on one foot with a finger raised, for instance—and if he had they could then run wiring up through him, stick a light bulb in his mouth, and turn him into a lamp.

The flashlights bobbed toward the building, and Grofield watched them, knowing he couldn't get to it before them, and even if he could it wouldn't do him any good. He was unarmed, a condition he doubted they shared.

Still, there was nowhere else to go. He plodded forward, moving more slowly now to give them a chance to get inside the building before he arrived.

But they weren't going in, at least not at first. He stopped again and watched, and saw one of the flashlights disappear while the other one bobbed along beside the building. The other one eventually appeared again at the back of the building, and the two flashlights came together once more.

Checking for tracks. Being sure he wasn't already inside. Grofield didn't like them at all.

The flashlights moved together now, and suddenly disappeared again. And then lights began going on, in the middle of the building at first, and then spreading out both to left and right, until every ground floor window was gleaming. And then nothing more happened at all.

It wasn't until he moved again that Grofield realized how numb his feet were getting. And his ears weren't tingling any more either. His fingers had become more painful, but they too would soon be numb if he stayed out here in the cold.

And there was still nowhere else to go but this building dead ahead. The others were full of people, but in this one there were only two. And both dressed for the outdoors. With any luck, one of them would have boots that would fit Grofield.

He moved forward again, and his body seemed heavier than it had ever been before. It was an effort to get the muscles to work, to make them lift a foot, move it forward, set it down again, shift

the arms and shoulders to shift the weight so the other foot could
be lifted, all of it heavy work, almost too much to do. It would be
so much easier just to stand where he was. Nothing much hurt
any more except his fingers and his throat when he inhaled
through his mouth, and those aches would soon go away.

It was amazing how fast it happened, how easily a person
could find a spot on his own native planet in which human life
was impossible. He was being killed by temperature, silently and
not too very painfully and very very quickly. He had to get angry
at himself to keep himself in motion, angry at Colonel Rahgos
and Vivian and Marba and General Pozos and Ken and even
Laufman, the driver who'd loused up the getaway from the
armored-car job and got him into this mess in the first place.
Anger was a good fuel, it kept him warm enough to move, it gave
him the determination to survive this mess somehow and spit
icicles in everybody's eyes.

There were no windows near the corner of the building, very
little light-spill there. Grofield staggered forward, his feet now
plowing a furrow through the snow, too heavy to be lifted up
over the snow, and when he got to the wall of the building he
sagged against it and just breathed for a while.

He closed his eyes too, and that was almost a fatal mistake.
Happily he wasn't balanced right against the wall, so when he
started to fall over he woke up again, startled, realizing he'd lost
consciousness, not knowing for how long, knowing only that if
he'd been propped more securely against the wall he never would
have awakened again.

No. It wasn't going to happen, he was damned if he was going
to let it happen. Could he allow himself to be so easily gotten rid
of? They put him out for the night, and it's all over.

He inched along the wall to his left, supporting a part of his
weight on the wall, and when he came to the first window he
peered cautiously in.

It was a storage room, with rough wooden partitions and rough wooden shelves full of cardboard cartons. The room was empty, but the door opposite the window stood open, with a well-lit hall outside and another open door beyond leading to another lit-up storage room. Grofield nodded, explaining to himself what he was seeing in an attempt to keep himself awake, and moved on.

All the windows looked into similar storage cubicles with open doors facing the same hall and more storage rooms on the far side. Halfway along the wall there was a door, with glass panes in the upper half, and looking through that Grofield could see a short hall leading to the central hall, and sitting in there were two black men, on kitchen chairs, facing in opposite directions, looking down the hall to left and right. They had machine guns on their laps, and they were smoking, and their heavy mackinaws were hanging open. They both wore high leather boots.

Grofield moved away from the door again, leaned against the wall, and began to mumble to himself. "All right," he muttered. "Let's wake up and think about this thing. The other half of the building is gonna be the same as this half. Right? Right. The way they've got it set up, I can't get in without them hearing me or seeing me. All these windows are going to be locked, so if I break one they'll hear it and they'll know where I am. Right? Right. So there's no way in. Right? Wrong. What do you mean, wrong? I mean, there's got to be a way in because I need a way in."

He stopped mumbling and stood there trying to think. There was less feeling in his fingers now, and the backs of his knees were hurting. His neck seemed stiff. His mind seemed stiff and fuzzy and full of glue and cobwebs.

He said, "Second floor." He looked up, and faintly he could see windows up there, but dark. They hadn't concerned themselves with the second floor, which meant they didn't believe it possible for him to get in up there, and they probably knew more about this place than he did.

Still, it was worth checking out. He didn't see any way to climb up along this wall, so he made himself move again, going on down toward the far end of the building to check out the other sides.

The other end of the building was mostly given over to one large storage area full of machinery, plows, and other mechanized devices, with an overhead door on the end wall. Grofield blundered along past this door, glancing in through the small window in its middle and seeing that an open space had been left down the center of the garage area, with an open door at the end leading to the corridor. He could plainly see the two of them sitting at their ease way down there in the middle of the corridor. Warm, comfortable, alert, well-armed. He hated them both.

He kept on moving, and at the end of the long door his hand bumped into a projection on the wall. He frowned at it and saw it was a metal box with a button on the front. A doorbell beside a garage door?

No, of course not. The garage door must be operated electrically, and this button would open it.

Wouldn't it be nice to push the button and watch the door slide up and then walk into the cozy warm inside of the building? Wouldn't it?

He pushed on, miserable, freezing. His eyelashes were weighted with ice, it was increasingly hard to see anything. He got to the corner of the building and then stopped and looked back.

Maybe?

Maybe.

He worked his way back again to the door, and studied it more closely. It wasn't the hinged, faceted type, it was all in one solid piece. When the button was pushed, it would swing up and out while the top part was sliding backward into the building.

He looked up at the second floor. Windows, dark and empty.

Was it possible? There were handles on the door. If he could push the button and then stand on one of the low handles, would it then be possible to ride the door up to the second floor and then get off the damn thing before it slid inside? Get off onto the narrow window sill up there, hang on some way, and get the damn window open. Quietly. With earnest prayers that he would find it unlocked.

A very wild notion, all in all, even if he'd been in the peak of condition, which he wasn't. But what else did he have going? And if it didn't work, there was still a chance he could get away into the darkness again before they got here from where they were sitting. A small chance.

Everything was a small chance at the moment, and this was the only thing that looked even remotely possible, so the hell with it. He reached out his numb thumb and pushed the button.

A loud door. The engine whirred and whined like a derrick, while Grofield scrambled to get one foot on the handle and press himself face forward against the rising door. The racket the motor was making, and the slowness of the door's rising, might both be caused by the addition of his extra weight. But at least the door was going up.

But Grofield wasn't. His clothing was covered with ice, his body was half-frozen and clumsy, and he just couldn't get his knees up under himself. He struggled and struggled while the door went up, but the metal surface was slippery under him, and he just wasn't going to get anywhere.

And the door was headed inside. Squinting up ahead of himself he saw the top of the door frame coming, saw that it would just clear him, and resigned himself to not getting to that second-story window. What was apparently going to happen, assuming he didn't get caught now, was that he would ride the door into the building and then back out again.

Feeling ridiculous and holding on tight, Grofield rode the door until it jolted to a stop, horizontal, just under the garage ceiling. Footsteps went by beneath him, and it sounded like only one pair. So they were smart, they sent only one man down here to check out the opening of the door, while the other one kept at his post in case it was meant as a distraction.

It was warm in here, in comparison with outside. He could smell the nice oily smell of an electric motor. He could feel how badly his body craved to stay indoors. He was waking up enough to understand just how close to the end he was out there. He wasn't dressed for that kind of weather, not his feet, not his head, not his hands.

It would take a minute or two for the guard to assure himself that Grofield wasn't around, and then he'd lower the door again. While waiting, Grofield lifted his head a little and looked around.

Not much to see. Two-by-twelve joists running from left to right, with the upstairs flooring set on them. Just ahead, the motor for the door, mounted on a solid iron framework suspended from the joists. To both sides, the metal tracks for the door.

Without thinking twice about it, Grofield crawled forward over the door, moving as silently as he could, his icy clothing slipping noiselessly over the metal of the door. He reached out and closed his hand around the nearest part of the motor's framework, and pulled himself forward, off the door and onto the framework. The iron strips were about three inches wide, and when he was done he was lying face down beside the motor, his thighs resting on one strip and his chest resting on the other. He lifted his feet—they were almost too heavy to lift—and wedged them into the angles between joists and upstairs flooring. He tucked his hands inside the front of his overcoat, between the buttons, so his arms wouldn't dangle down. Nothing dangled down now but his head, and that not very far.

He was now propped into an odd but not really uncomfortable position, face down, hands tucked inside coat, knees bent, feet up behind him and jammed against the flooring above, head drooped forward so he was looking upside down back along the length of himself at the door he'd just crawled off.

That door didn't move for another three or four minutes, and then suddenly it did, and a man came walking in from outside, stamping snow off his boots. He stood directly under Grofield and called something incomprehensible to his partner down there in the corridor. Then he turned back and watched the door while it finished curving out and down and at last snicked shut, after which he shifted his machine gun from the ready position to the over-the-forearm carrying position and walked away to the corridor, going back to his chair and his partner.

Grofield just lay where he was. It was warm in here, delicious, it must have been fifty-five or sixty up here at the top of the room where the heat collected. It was really beautiful. Grofield lay there, totally relaxed, his position slightly cramped but not too bad, and he felt how beautiful it was to be indoors, and his eyes slowly closed, and very gently he went to sleep.

TWENTY

GROFIELD AWOKE THINKING he was an astronaut. Tendrils of confused dreams ran mistlike through his mind, an image of himself as an astronaut floating in his bulky suit outside the ship, and when he opened his eyes he saw he was really flying. A concrete floor was way below him, he was flying just under the ceiling, flying along . . .

He started, recoiled, slapped the back of his head against the floorboards above his head. That concrete was real down there! For one awful second he felt himself falling, and he struggled his hands free from his coat, shoving them out ahead of him, splay-fingered, in the instinctive movement of breaking one's fall.

But then he saw the concrete was getting no closer, and he felt the ache of something pressing against his chest, something else digging into the front of his thighs. He kicked his feet loose from where they'd been wedged, and the knees complained at the movement, shooting pains up and down his legs.

Good God, what a mess. Comprehension was returning to him, coming in with the awareness of his various aches and pains, and a great black feeling of hopelessness washed over him, leaving him bitter and pessimistic.

Look where he was. Hanging from the goddamn ceiling, stuck up here like a butterfly on a drying board. And if he were to try to lower himself to the ground he'd be right in plain view of those two bastards in the hallway.

Could he stay here? No, dammit. In the morning they'd be searching for him, they'd probably be coming in and out of this garage. There were a couple of skimobiles down there, little open scooters with skis in front and treads in back, and they'd probably use them to look for him tomorrow. Sooner or later someone would look up and see him.

But what else could he do? He'd bought himself an extra few hours of life by getting in here, but he'd slept them away. He was warm now, but even more stiff than before. And just as hopeless.

He shifted position, trying to find some fairly bearable way to lie here, but there wasn't any. In moving around, though, he banged his elbow against the motor, adding one more pain to the catalog. He gave the motor a dirty look, and then gave it a more careful look.

An electric motor. If he could cause a short-circuit in that and blow the fuse, maybe the lights in here would go out, and give him a shot at dropping unseen to the floor. Then he could hide in with the equipment down there and see what happened next.

It was better than just hanging around, so what the hell. He hunched himself a little closer to the motor, till he was nearly wrapped around it, and gave it some close scrutiny.

That should be it, right there, a pair of wires that emerged from a box in the ceiling and attached to screws on the top rear of the motor. If he could cross those wires—without electrocuting himself—the motor and some fuse somewhere should both go blooey.

So what he needed was metal. Any on his person? None, naturally. He looked around on the motor for anything that looked both loose and unessential, but there wasn't anything. The framework he was sharing with the motor also had no usable spare parts. He looked up, mostly to give God a long-suffering look, and saw nails sticking out of the floorboards above his head. Here and there throughout the room nails had been driven in from above, maybe something to do with partitions up there, and some of them stuck down more than an inch on the underside.

One of the nice long ones was just within reach. Grofield took off his right glove and reached out and up, grasping the nail between thumb and forefinger. He pulled, slowly bending the nail this way. It didn't want to come, but he was insistent, and when he had it at about a forty-five-degree angle he pushed it away again. Then pulled it back, pushed it away, pulled it back. The longer he did it the easier it got, and the nail became warm against his finger and thumb, and then hot, and then just about too hot to touch, and then at long long last it snapped, and he was left holding a piece of nail about one and one-quarter inch long.

Now was the tricky part. He didn't want to go through all this clever stuff and then zap himself. Being extremely careful, he rested the sharp point of the nail against one of the two screws holding the wire on the top of the motor. He had the point nested in the groove of the screw, and angled the screw so it would, with any luck, fall over onto the other screw. He bit his lower lip, held his breath, moved his feet up so they were against the iron strip down there and he was ready to drop the instant darkness fell, he licked his lips, swallowed, let the nail go, it fell on the other screw, and the door began to open.

Would nothing work right? He was so exasperated he almost asked the question aloud. First he'd tried to ride the garage door to the second floor and wound up hanging from the first-floor ceiling. Now all he'd wanted to do was blow one stinking fuse, and here came the door again.

Also one of the guards. Grofield heard him running down the corridor in this direction.

It was irritation more than anything else that guided what he did next. He grabbed his chest-support iron strip in both hands, kicked loose from the other strip, swung down like Tarzan out of a tree, and as the guard came running in Grofield kicked him in the face with both feet.

The guard did a very interesting thing. While his feet proceeded to run up an imaginary hill, his head fell backward, so that for one insane instant he was lying horizontal in midair, a good four feet off the floor, as though he'd been left there by an absentminded magician. But then Grofield's tired hands lost their grip on the length of iron, he sat on the guard's stomach, and the two of them fell to the floor, the guard breaking Grofield's fall.

The machine gun, the machine gun, the machine gun. The guard had come in toting the thing at port arms, and it had gone flying somewhere when Grofield had turned violent. Now Grofield scrambled around in a frantic circle on the unconscious guard's stomach, looking for it, and saw it just hitting the floor a little past the guard's feet. He lunged for it, got it in both hands, rolled over onto his back, stared down past his feet at the doorway and the corridor, and saw the guard down there just spinning around to see what the racket was.

Grofield showed the machine gun but didn't fire it, hoping to avoid unnecessary noise and bloodshed—he might want that mackinaw—but the guard didn't feel the same way. He fired a quick burst, but he made the mistake most people make when firing at something below them, and the bullets zipped over Grofield's head, skinned the concrete behind him, and bounced out into the snow.

Oh, all right. Grofield squeezed the trigger, the gun in his hands chattered, and the guard down there jolted backward over the two chairs and crumpled up on the floor.

Grofield rolled to his right, got to knees and elbows, and was stuck there for a while. He couldn't go any farther until he let go of the machine gun. Then he could push his torso upward so that he was kneeling on the concrete beside the unconscious guard, facing the open doorway. The door was just snicking into place in the open position.

Grofield looked out at the cold darkness. He could see two of the other buildings, with fewer lights lit now. Both of them were a good distance away. Had the firing been heard? Two short bursts, both indoors, they probably hadn't been. In any case it was a chance he would have to take.

And here came the door. It had opened all the way, stopped briefly, made clicking and grinding noises, and now it was closing again. That was nice.

Grofield leaned carefully forward and picked up the machine gun and used it as a crutch to get himself to his feet, getting all the way up at about the same time the door was getting all the way down. He stood there leaning against the machine gun and watched the door shut. It made clicking and grinding noises. It started to open again.

Oh, damn it to hell. Grofield looked around in exasperation, and an A ladder was leaning against the wall to the right. He went around a skimobile and a small dozer, wrapped his arms around the ladder, and staggered back with it. He had a great deal of trouble opening it, and a great deal of reluctance climbing it, and during that time the door just kept opening and closing, being on its fourth round trip when he finally started up the ladder.

Talk about signals. Anybody glancing casually out a window in any of those other buildings would see the yellow doorway constantly contracting and expanding, contracting and expanding, and sooner or later it would occur to somebody to send an army over here and find out how come.

He got up the ladder just as the door was coming up again, but then he didn't want to touch the nail with his hand so he hurried back down again and found a crumpled cigarette pack in the unconscious guard's mackinaw pocket. He carried them up the ladder as the door was starting down again and used the pack to push the nail off the screws. It rolled off the motor entirely and plinked onto the concrete.

Grofield stayed on the ladder, watching the door mistrustfully. It scooped out and down, it closed, it clicked, it stopped. Grofield smiled.

He climbed down the ladder and went over to check the guard he'd kicked and sat on, and he was completely out, though breathing. And he was wearing fine-looking leather boots, knee-high.

It was the first time in his criminal career that Grofield had stolen the shoes from an unconscious man. It made him feel like a Skid Row mugger, but this was no time for professional snobbery. He removed the boots and the socks underneath them, and then took off his own cold wet shoes and socks. Sitting on the concrete floor, he used the guy's shirt to dry his feet, then put on the long woolen socks and slipped his feet into the boots, smiling in almost drunken delight at the discovery that they were fur-lined.

They fit. A little big, maybe, but that was better than the shoes he'd been wearing, which had been a little too small to begin with and hadn't improved by being soaked. The guard's mackinaw was more practical than Grofield's overcoat, so he made that switch too, then picked up the machine gun and walked down the corridor to see what the other one looked like.

He was dead. Grofield took his machine gun, but kept away from the body. On the floor near the overturned chairs, though, he found fur-lined caps and gloves and four more clips of ammunition for the machine guns. He carried these back to the garage and put them on the floor there, then took the guard under the armpits and dragged him into the corridor and into an empty storage cubicle to the right. He went back and got the laces out of his shoes and used them to tie the guard's ankles and wrists together. Then he shut and locked the door and went on to investigate the rest of the building.

It was beautiful. All the supplies were stored in here, food and drink, cleaning supplies, cans of gasoline and oil, light bulbs, everything. He found a can opener, opened a can of beef stew, and ate it cold, with his fingers.

For the half hour after that he was very busy, searching in room after room, picking out the things he thought he might want, carrying them to the garage and leaving them on the floor there. When he was finished he had assembled canned food, waterproofed matches, gasoline, blankets, and a flashlight. He then pulled one of the skimobiles over and began loading it up. It had two seats, one behind the other, and he loaded the equipment onto the rear seat and the floor, lashing it all on with rope, everything but one machine gun and the flashlight. He checked the skimobile's gas tank, and it was full. He pulled on his gloves and was ready.

There was another button on the inside wall, beside the door. Grofield pushed it and the door slid up and he rolled the skimobile out into the snow. He pushed the outside button to shut the door again, then started the skimobile's engine, shifted into forward, and the little snow scooter obediently snicked off, gliding over the snow he'd had so much trouble with before.

He took a long curve around to the right, away from the cluster of buildings, and then just went straight. From time to time he'd look over his shoulder to be sure he was still headed away from the lodge, but otherwise he squinted into the faint starlit darkness ahead, traveling over rolling snow hills, all alone, without even trees around to keep him company.

If only he knew what the North Star looked like, he could do his purposeful traveling right now, but he was no navigator. He'd have to wait until the beginning of dawn. As soon as he saw where on the horizon the light first appeared he would have a good approximation of which way was south. Until then, travel would be pointless.

Except to keep clear of the people at the lodge, of course. That's why he was headed outward now. He could be going due north for all he knew—he hoped not—but the important thing was that he was going away. It would be morning before they could really begin to track him, and by then he'd be on his way south, clear of that crazy bunch forever.

Ken would still be a problem, of course, but a problem that would keep for a while. Sufficient unto the night, etc.

After a while he stopped. The last couple of times he'd looked back he hadn't seen their lights at all, there were too many intervening snow dunes. He should be far enough away now to be safe until dawn.

He'd stopped in a low spot, protected from the slight icy breeze. He got two of the blankets, lay them down on top of one another in the snow, stretched out on top of them, and rolled himself in them, covering himself completely from the bottom of his feet up to his nose. His fur cap was pulled down low, covering ears and forehead, and he lay on his side, curled up slightly, and waited for morning.

TWENTY-ONE

GUNFIRE.

Grofield had been dozing, warm and comfortable inside his cocoon of blankets, his stomach working away contentedly on another can of cold beef stew, and only gradually did he become aware of the faint sounds, rattle and chatter and brief bark.

He sat up, frowning, listening. The sound was far away, and it came in spurts, with uneasy silences in between. A battle of some kind, an honest-to-God battle.

Where else but at the lodge?

Grofield pushed away the blankets and got to his feet, and now he could see a murky red smudge on the horizon, far away in the direction from which he'd come.

What now? Were they burning the place down?

Could it be Ken? Rescue? Had the sons of bitches put a transmitter inside his body after all?

He didn't know, under the circumstances, if the idea was repulsive or not.

In any case, he had to know what was going on. It might be

nothing more than a falling-out among the members of that charming bunch back there, but whatever it was there was just a chance there was advantage for him in it.

He folded up the blankets, tied everything onto the skimobile again, slung the machine gun over his shoulder, started the engine and headed toward the flickering red glow on the horizon.

After he'd traveled a couple of minutes he came up over the top of a snow dune and all at once could see the fire. It was huge, one entire building was aflame, one of the two dormitory buildings, and in the red light Grofield could see confused activity around the other buildings, rushing about, savage but incomprehensible motion.

He steered to the right, angling around the buildings, trying to see without being seen. It turned out he had been directly opposite the lake where their plane had landed yesterday afternoon, and when he'd circled far enough to see the lake there was another plane there now, its single floodlight glaring toward the front of the lodge, outlining it in white light, with the red flames behind it and to its left.

Was it really Ken? There was no one at all in the floodlit area in front of the lodge, all the activity taking place behind it, in the uncertain red light of the fire. The plane, in the darkness behind its light, was just a black blur with no legible markings. But if it wasn't Ken, or some of Ken's associates, it was surely *somebody* who'd attacked Rahgos and Pozos and Company, and Grofield's feeling right now was that any enemy of that bunch was a friend of his.

Maybe. There was no point being foolhardy about it. Grofield therefore didn't approach the plane directly but angled off behind it, the skimobile chugging away across the snow-covered ice on a long curve that would bring him to the plane from the rear.

The skimobile wasn't exactly silent, its engine being perhaps a little more quiet than a power mower, but the racket from behind the lodge more than covered the noise of Grofield's approach. Aside from the roar of the flames back there, a surprisingly loud

and threatening sound, there was the intermittent crackle of gunfire, and occasional shouts and yelps and screams from the people
involved. Under all that noise Grofield made his wide circle out
across the lake and came in from behind the plane, seeing it now
silhouetted against the spotlit shore. It was either the same two-
engine cargo plane he'd come up here in or another one just like
it. If it was the same one, what would that mean? Intramural
combat, maybe.

He was almost to the tail of the plane when two men came
running around the corner of the lodge, pistols in their hands.
They ran toward the plane, bent low, though no one pursued
them so far as Grofield could see, and as they neared the plane
another man swung down from the open door midway in the
fuselage and hurried forward to meet them.

That one was familiar, the one who'd been in the plane. The
silhouette rang some sort of bell with Grofield, he wasn't sure
why. The three men stopped near the wingtip and conversed
quickly with one another, shouting to be heard, waving their
arms. The language wasn't English. Grofield was no expert, but it
seemed to him the language was at least similar to the one spoken
by the man who'd killed Henry Carlson.

Why was that one guy familiar? Who the hell was he? Grofield
got off the skimobile and trotted forward to the plane, then
moved cautiously along beside it, coming up the opposite side
from where the three men were talking. When he reached the
wing he bent and looked under the fuselage at them gesticulating
away over there, and the familiar one was the doctor who'd
helped kidnap him. Bushy mustache and everything. Shouting in
a language that wasn't English and wasn't French.

Le Quebecois? This was a hell of a place to start an armed re-
volt. There had to be another explanation.

And a better time to look for it. Grofield unshipped his machine gun and trotted back toward the skimobile, checking over
his shoulder as he ran, but no one saw him. He got onto the

skimobile and steered it away from there, out over the lake away from the noise and light.

He didn't know what the fight was about, but he did know now that both sides meant trouble for him, so the best thing for him to do was get way off on the sidelines and wait for it to be over, rooting for both teams to score a knockout. In the morning he'd see if there was anything useful to him left in the shambles. Like a compass, for instance, a compass would be nice.

He was thinking about compasses, and traveling south, and hot showers, when he saw the muzzle flash ahead of him and a second later felt something burn the top of his left shoulder. He dropped off the seat at once, onto the ice, and rolled so he was on his stomach, with the machine gun in his hands. The skimobile traveled a few yards farther, losing momentum, then stopped and stalled.

Grofield lay unmoving, knowing he was silhouetted against the light behind him. He stared into the darkness in front of him, but the light source was too far away, there was nothing to be seen.

Footsteps, crunching on the snow. Grofield kept his head down, listened to them coming closer. He held tight to the gun.

He was just about to roll over and start firing when he saw the green ski pants, no more than six feet away. He hesitated, and she came another step forward, and instead of firing he lunged upward all at once, swinging the butt of the machine gun around at her knees, hearing and feeling it hit, and she screamed and toppled over as though a rug had been pulled out from underneath her. Grofield leaped forward and swept the automatic from her hand, while his other hand reached for her throat. She was all done up in fur coat, fur collar, fur hat with fur straps under the chin, he couldn't get through all that hair to her neck. She squirmed and wriggled and punched at him with gloved fists, and finally all he could think of to do was grab the fur hat and thump her head a couple of times against the ice.

The fight went out of her at once, her arms dropping to her

sides, and a glazed look came into her eyes. Grofield got his machine gun, stood up, found the automatic in the snow. He tapped it against his side to shake off the snow, and put it in his mackinaw pocket, then turned and walked over to the skimobile. He was getting onto it when she called his name. He looked over and could barely make out the shape of her, sitting up now. Bitterly she was saying, "Why don't you finish the job? Are you going to let your friends kill me?"

"They aren't my friends," Grofield said. "If you mean that bunch that's attacking your bunch, they're not my friends at all."

There was a little silence. He couldn't see her face, so after a few seconds he shrugged and turned to start the engine again, but then she said, "I don't believe you."

"I always run away from my friends," he said, and started the engine.

"Wait! Please, wait!"

He turned in irritation, looking in her general direction. "Wait for what?"

"I thought they were your people, that's why I shot at you. I wouldn't have shot at you if I'd known."

"I'll bear that in mind," Grofield said, and prepared to shift into forward.

"Don't! Listen to me, please!"

Why didn't he just leave her here? Hadn't she shot at him? Hadn't she turned that tin-star Colonel against him? But he remembered that look of doubt in her face just before he'd gone out the window, and the frantic shooing gestures she'd made when he was down below in the snow, and he hesitated. And then he thought, if she was really in bad straits, with no one left to turn to but him, it was possible he could exchange protection for information, and find out at last just what all of this had been about. And wouldn't that make Ken happy, assuming he ever saw Ken or civilization or anything at all ever again.

So he switched off the engine and said, "All right, I'll listen."

She had gotten to her feet, and limped now over to him, favoring the leg he'd hit with the gun barrel. She said, "I need your help. And it isn't just me, it's everybody."

"Not too close," Grofield warned her. "That's close enough right there. I can see you, and you can't touch me."

"I won't try anything," she said. "I thought those were your people attacking us, or I never would have shot at you."

"You said that."

"I couldn't understand the Americans behaving like that," she said. "Just shooting and killing and setting the place on fire. I couldn't understand it."

"They aren't Americans," Grofield told her. "I don't know who they are."

"They can't get their hands on . . ." She stopped, moving her head back and forth in urgency and frustration. "We've got to stop them," she said. "You've got to help me."

"You mean, considering all I owe you?"

She said, "I didn't mean for you to be killed, not ever. I thought you'd be locked up again. You did that yourself, you refused to be locked up, you forced the Colonel to decide to kill you. All I wanted was for you to be locked away somewhere."

"Thanks."

"Because I didn't trust you," she said. "And be fair, be honest, I had a right not to trust you. You wanted to go poking your nose around, that's why you were so set against being locked up. Isn't it?"

"I could have been kept from seeing things I shouldn't," Grofield said.

"You're too sneaky," she said. "I'm trying to be honest with you now. I'm sorry for the way it worked out, I didn't know you'd be silly enough to give the Colonel an ultimatum like that, but I was right to argue against letting you go free."

Grofield shook his head and grinned. "You're such a sweet-talker," he said. "I swear you're turning my head."

She said, "But I *didn't* want you to die. At the end there, I wanted to say something, but it was just impossible. You had put the Colonel into a position where he had no choice, not without feeling humiliated."

Grofield nodded. "I admit I misjudged that situation," he said. "I thought a respectful but egalitarian approach would do the job."

"You argued with him," she said, and she sounded faintly shocked still at the memory of it.

"What I should have done was tug my forelock, huh?"

"What you should have done," she said, "was admit that you were lost without his protection and beg him to help you. Everyone likes to be in a position to do magnanimous favors, the Colonel's just as human as anybody else."

"Is he? We just pretend he's divine, is that it?"

"For someone who ignores his country," she said, "you're far too American for your own good."

"Maybe." He glanced back at the lodge and the plane and the battle, the sounds of which seemed now to be fading somewhat. He looked at the girl again and said, "Is that what you wanted to tell me? About the national traits embedded in my behavior patterns?"

She suddenly remembered the urgency she was feeling, and said quickly, "We have to do something to stop them. If they're not Americans, God knows who they are or who hired them. They can't take . . ." She stopped, seemed to cast around for another way to say it, started again: "There are four metal canisters somewhere in the lodge," she said. "They must not get their hands on them, those people, they must not get them away from here."

"Why? What's in them?"

"I—I can't tell you exactly. It's a weapon, it's a very dangerous thing. We can't let it fall into the wrong hands."

"If it's a dangerous weapon," Grofield said, "it was already in the wrong hands. What is this weapon?"

"I honestly can't tell you."

"Then I honestly can't help you," Grofield said. "Good-bye, Vivian, it's been varied."

"Wait!"

He waited, watching her. He could see the indecision on her face, despite the darkness. He didn't help, he just waited, and finally she said, "It's germs."

"It's what?"

"Disease germs," she said. "Laboratory produced disease germs."

"You mean like in germ warfare?"

"Yes," she said.

"For God's sake! What kind of—"

"Look!"

He looked. The plane was turning around. Way back there it was ponderously wheeling about, and as he watched, the floodlight hit him square in the eye.

TWENTY-TWO

GROFIELD SAID, "Could they have the canisters so soon?"

"No, it's impossible, they're hidden. Only a few people even know where they are. And I've been watching, and only one man got on that plane. Not carrying anything."

"Going back to report," Grofield said. "Climb on the back here. It won't be comfortable, but it's the best I've got."

"What are you going to do?"

"Get the hell away from here before that plane arrives," Grofield told her. "It's coming this way, in case you hadn't noticed."

There was more light now, with the plane's beam facing this way, and he could see the startled look that crossed her face. "Oh! Yes!" She clambered onto the pile of goods stacked on the skimobile's rear seat, clutching Grofield's shoulders to hold herself steady.

"You set?"

"I think so."

He started off, heading at an angle to the left, the more quickly to get out of range of the plane's light, and everything would probably have been all right if they hadn't hit the bump, a jagged step caused by an old buckling of the ice. But they did hit it, hard, and the machine jolted, bouncing Grofield up and down and throwing Vivian completely away. He heard her yelp, felt her hands leave his shoulders, and when he had the skimobile under control again and looked back she was lying on the ice back there, just starting to roll over and get up.

He wheeled around, making as tight a turn as he could, and saw beyond her the plane trundling this way, coming uncomfortably fast. And how her green ski pants stood out against the surrounding darkness.

They stood out too well, in fact, because just as Grofield pulled to a stop beside her and started to help her aboard again the plane suddenly veered, bathing them in direct light.

"I'm sorry!" she shouted.

"Wrap your arms around my chest!" he yelled back. "If you go again, you'll have to take me with you!"

She half sat and half knelt on the pile of provisions, her arms around his chest from behind, and he scooted the skimobile around in another tight turn and began to run away from the plane.

But not fast enough. He could see the light getting brighter and brighter around him, see their shadow getting shorter and shorter out in front of him. He could even hear the roar of the plane over their own noises, and he already knew it when she screamed in his ear, "They're on top of us!"

"Hold on, for Christ's sake!" he shouted back, and veered sharply to the left. Out of the corner of his eye he could see the lumbering wing, like the wing of a huge predatory bird, so close he nearly passed under it. For a few seconds he was heading into darkness, and then the light swung into place behind them again. But not so close as it had been before they'd swerved. So the plane was faster, but the skimobile was more maneuverable, so maybe the only question now was which of them would run out of gas first, and he had an unhappy feeling he knew the answer to that one.

Then she let him know that wasn't the only question after all, because she yelled in his ear, "They're shooting at us!"

"How do you know?"

"I see the flashes! They're shooting out the window in the pilot's compartment. A pistol, I think."

"Make yourself small," he suggested. "And hold on, we're going to the right this time."

"I'm holding."

She was, too, almost too hard for him to breathe, but this was no time for minor adjustments. He said nothing, just veered to the right, and once again was rewarded with a few seconds of relative darkness before the light gleamed on his back once again.

But he couldn't go on like this, dammit, being chased all over the lake by an airplane. If they ever did catch up, they'd just run him down, but in the meantime they could score a hit with one of their pistol shots, and in the long run he'd wind up out of gas. So something had to be done.

All right, what did he have? He thought about the equipment he had lashed to the back seat, and briefly considered somehow turning one of the spare cans of gasoline into a Molotov cocktail, but the acrobatics involved in getting it out from under Vivian while they zigged and zagged around the lake seemed prohibitive, so he reluctantly abandoned the idea. It would be nice, though, to blow the damn plane up.

All that was needed, actually, was to get away from it. Let it fly away, about that he didn't care. And if somehow he could get to the shore, that would be the end of the chase. The plane could follow him around out here on this flat ballroom floor, but on the rolling hills of soft snow ashore the plane couldn't possibly go. They'd have to take off, and at night they'd have a hell of a time finding him from the air. So the object of the game was to find a shore somewhere.

And meantime, the plane was getting closer again. He shouted, "Hold on!" and veered to the right once more. But this time, instead of just going off at a forty-five degree angle, he kept around in a tight U-turn, knowing he could turn well inside the plane's turning radius. He saw the distant red smudge that was the fire at the lodge, and kept turning, shouting to Vivian, "Let me know when the fire's directly behind us!"

"All right!"

He could see the plane's tail assembly to his right now, the plane being very cumbersome at this business of turning a complete circle. He clenched his teeth and leaned into the curve and kept going around.

"Behind us!"

He nodded briskly and straightened out, and shot away, leaving the plane barely more than halfway around its own turn.

"Oh good good good!" she was yelling. "Oh they're way back! Oh you're beautiful beautiful beautiful!"

"Stop hitting me on the head!" he yelled. "Hold on or you'll fall off again!"

So she held on, and Grofield leaned over the handlebars, and when at last the plane's light picked them up again it was no more than a gray smudge. Crofield smiled into the rushing darkness, knowing he'd found the slingshot for this Goliath. The bigger they are, they harder they turn. The plane might catch up with them again, but he'd just pull the same stunt and be on his way again. And sooner or later he'd have to find this goddamn lake's farther shore. After all, every lake in the world has a farther shore. Even oceans have farther shores.

"It's getting closer again!" she hollered.

"I know! I can see the light!"

He let it get very close this time, he could hear the roaring down the back of his neck, and then he made the sharp turn again, this time going under the wingtip as he curved around. He leaned into it, feeling good, knowing he'd outfoxed them, and then she yelled, "They aren't coming after us!"

He risked a look, almost losing his balance, and she was right. The plane was still trundling on in the same direction, hurrying away from them now, picking up speed.

"They gave up!" she yelled, and pummeled his shoulders.

"They did not! Hold on!"

He knew what they were up to now, the bastards. Why wouldn't they accept defeat? Spoilsports. Rotters. What if Goliath had gotten up and taken two Excedrin and gone back into the fight? What then?

He made the turn so tight this time they nearly flipped over, and then he chased after the plane, straightening out onto his former course just in time to see the plane lifting into the air, far away, and its light still not illuminating anything that looked like a farther shore.

Was this the goddamn ocean? Was he on his way to Iceland? For God's sake, enough was enough.

He hunched over, urging the little machine on, and Vivian clung to his torso, her head against his head, the fur fringe of her hat tickling his cheek. She shouted, "What are they going to do?"

"Wait and see!"

The plane was up now, circling into the sky, no longer awkward and bulky and cumbersome. It was in its own element now, and had become fast and lethal. Grofield, taking quick glances up as he raced now into unrelieved black darkness, saw the plane climb and climb, circling, and knew it would only be a few seconds before it started its run. He shouted, "Let me know when it starts down!"

"Are they going to land on us?"

"Only if they don't have anything in there to drop, honey."

She didn't have anything to say to that, but a few seconds later she cried, "Here they come!"

"Hold on!" he yelled, and began swerving the machine back and forth.

"They're shooting!"

Grofield concentrated on his driving, seeing the spotlight giving him a shadow again, seeing it get brighter. He kept swerving out of it, but it kept picking him up again, and when it seemed to him the last possible instant he made a hard left and the plane roared by no more than twenty feet in the air and something blew up on his old route.

"Wonderful!" he yelled. "They've got hand grenades in there!" He swerved back to the right, and kept going.

She yelled, "What can we do?"

"Pray for shore!"

"They're coming around again! Give me your machine gun, I'll shoot them down!"

"Without falling off? Forget it!"

"They're going to *kill* us!"

"Don't you believe it!"

"Here they come! Oh here they come!"

The blackness ahead of him turned gray, paler, brighter, the long black shadow of their shape grew shorter, and abruptly he slammed on the brake, and she almost flipped over his head. He pushed back against her, to keep her aboard, and the plane growled by just over their heads, and there were two explosions, ahead of them, one to the left and one to the right. If he'd repeated the same maneuver as last time he would have run directly into one of those grenades.

"Will you warn me?" she bleated.

"No time. Hold on." And he accelerated again.

And this time, before the plane lifted, he saw in its light an unevenness ahead, a rising ragged slope of snow. The shore, at long long last.

Then the plane had lifted, was turning away, and there was no longer any light to see by. Grofield yelled, "We're going to hit the shore in a minute! For God's sake hold on!"

"I will!"

"Do you see the other machine gun tied on back there?"

"See it? It's been raping me for the last ten minutes!"

"When we stop, grab it and run to the left, and if the plane makes a try for us shoot the hell out of it."

"You bet I will!"

"Try to get . . . "

The machine hit something. It bounced into the air, Grofield lost the handlebars, Vivian's arms were torn away from around his chest, and he found himself flying through space with his feet somehow entangled with the machinery. He landed badly in soft snow, lunged off to the right, and the skimobile rolled over his feet and went on its own way.

Grofield struggled with the machine gun strapped to his shoulder, finally got hold of it, and light was starting again. He didn't know where Vivian was, he wanted to yell to her to shoot at the light, but he didn't know if she'd managed to get the other gun or not. He didn't even know if she was still conscious.

But here it came. He lifted up, and saw nothing but that glaring white spotlight screaming directly at him out of the black sky. An actor he might be, but he felt absolutely no urge to take a bow. He aimed the machine gun and began firing and the light shrieked closer, and suddenly it went out.

Grofield rolled into a tight ball, knowing retribution was coming. He shoved himself as deeply as possible into the snow, but when the blast did come it was damn close, and it shoved him even deeper. For the second time tonight the wind was knocked out of him, and for a few awful seconds he lay there with his mouth open, mouth and nose full of snow, finding himself absolutely incapable of taking a breath.

Breath came back slowly, with an agonizing pain in the chest, but it did come back. And the plane didn't. When he could move, Grofield rolled over onto his back, brushed the snow out of his eyes, and looked up. At first he saw nothing, but then he made out the receding red tail assembly light, high in the sky, going away, as though no longer interested in such petty problems as Alan Grofield.

He sat up, stiff and aching and bruised all over. He called, "Vivian?"

Somebody groaned.

He got to hands and knees. "Groan again," he called.

She groaned again.

He crawled in that direction, and touched wet cloth. He slid his hand along the cloth and said, "Vivian?"

A weak voice said, "Watch that hand, there."

"Why? What have I got?"

"So far, leg."

He patted it. "You sound like you're all right," he said. "Do you think you can stand on this?"

"In a day or two."

"We don't have a day or two."

"You're right." She grunted, and then her shoulder bumped into his face. "Sorry. I was sitting up."

"That's okay." He put a hand on her shoulder, slid it down her arm to her gloved hand. Then he got stiffly to his feet, and pulled her up.

She leaned against him briefly. "That was exhausting," she said.

"We have to find the skimobile," he said.

"I know." She stepped away, but still held his hand. "I have a flashlight," she said. "Do we dare use it?"

"Definitely. They've gone."

"I didn't get a chance at the machine gun," she said. "I'm sorry, it all happened so fast."

"It worked out."

Light, a narrow flashlight beam shining on churned-up snow. They were no more than six feet from the edge of the lake, and about a dozen feet in the other direction was the skimobile, tilted to the right, with a spray of blankets and canned goods all around it.

She was still holding Grofield's hand, and he saw her looking at him in the reflected glow from the flashlight. He said, "Let's go check out the damage."

"Sure," she said, but when he started forward she stood there, and kept holding his hand. He glanced back at her, puzzled, and she said, "Thank you."

"I was taking care of me, too," Grofield reminded her.

"You didn't have to take a passenger," she said. "Thank you."

"You're welcome," Grofield said.

TWENTY-THREE

GROFIELD SIGHED IN ANIMAL PLEASURE and threw the empty Spam can away. He scrubbed his hands clean in the snow, dried them as best he could on the blanket he had wrapped around himself, and put his gloves back on. "That," he said, "was good."

"Murm," she said.

It was pitch black, he couldn't see her at all. He said, "What was that?"

"My mouth wur full," she said, sounding as though it still was.

"Oh," he said. "Let me know when you're done, so we can talk."

"Murm."

They were sitting side by side in the darkness, both wrapped in blankets, their backs against the skimobile. While Vivian had held the flashlight he'd checked the machine out and found it still in good shape. Then he'd gathered the supplies together again, opened a few cans, and they'd sat down here to eat and rest.

It seemed there were fewer stars now, one whole segment of sky was now lightless, and the remainder didn't give enough light to matter. Far away across the lake the lights of the lodge looked like more stars, tiny and dim. The fire had died down over there now, there was no longer any redness to relieve the black at all.

"There!" she said. "That was good."

"You're done?"

"My hands are sticky."

"Clean them in the snow."

After a little silence she said, "Now they're wet."

"Dry them on your blanket."

Another little silence, and she said, "Fine." She touched his shoulder. "Would you mind if I leaned my head on you?"

"Can you talk with your head leaning?"

"Sure. You want to talk?"

"Definitely," he said.

Her head leaned against his shoulder. "All right. What do you want to talk about?"

"What's going on," he said.

"I'm sitting here with my head on your shoulder."

He didn't say anything.

She lifted her head, and he could tell she was trying to look at him in the darkness. She said, "Not funny?"

"Not funny," he agreed. "Mostly because I don't know how much time we have before that plane gets back. If they're only going as far as that lake we started from, they can do the round trip in two hours."

"All right," she said. "I don't know where the canisters are, I can't help you with that."

"I'm not ready to talk about the canisters yet," he said. "I want to start a heck of a lot earlier than that. Like this meeting. Tell me about it."

"There's nothing to tell. They came to bid for the canisters. Naturally, it was supposed—"

"Wait a second," Grofield said. "The canisters were for sale? They were being auctioned off?"

"Yes, of course."

"Who was doing the selling?"

"The people who had them."

"Come on, Vivian."

"Well, I'm sorry, that's who. They belonged to the United States Army to begin with, they were stolen from a storage depot somewhere in the States. Four Army men took them."

"*American* Army men?"

"Yes, of course."

"Where are these four guys?"

"At the lodge. If they aren't dead now."

"I didn't see any Americans there," Grofield said. "I was the only one."

"That's what's so charming about people like you," she said, some of the old coldness coming back into her voice. "You were the only *white* American there."

"They're Negroes? Four Negro soldiers?"

"What's the matter?"

"That shakes me a little," he said.

"I don't know what you're talking about."

"These days black men are supposed to be the heroes," he explained. "Never mind, let's hear the rest."

"There is no rest. They stole the canisters, they arranged for this place this weekend, they contacted nine governments—"

"I was told seven."

"American intelligence isn't infallible," she said drily. "Believe me, nine were invited and nine showed up."

"All Third World?"

"Naturally. And all unimportant enough so their leaders could safely travel incognito to a meeting in Canada."

"Why the leaders? Why not send representatives with power to purchase?"

"I can't speak for any other government," she said, "but I know my Colonel Rahgos wouldn't dare send anyone in his place to a meeting like this. Have that man return with a weapon like that, and with new contacts among the leaders of other nations? Colonel Rahgos became president of Undurwa after the army revolted and beheaded the last president, and most of the other leaders at this meeting came to power in similar ways, and they know just how tempting it would be for a representative here to go home and decide to take his president's place at home, too."

"Assuming his was the government that made the high bid," Grofield pointed out.

"What? Oh no, there wasn't to be only one high bidder. Price was to be discussed, each government was to decide how much it wanted, and everyone would get a part. There's enough in those four canisters to kill everyone on earth forty times."

"That's lovely," Grofield said. "What a goddamn sweet thing for everybody to be playing with."

"No one liked it," she said. "But no one could refuse the invitation. One never knows who will be one's friend tomorrow. What if Colongel Rahgos had decided not to come, not to bid, not to buy? One of the other purchasers is Dhaba, and we share a three-hundred-mile border with Dhaba. A lot of that border has never been exactly defined, and no one knows for sure what might yet be found in that area. Metals, or oil, or merely fertile land for our expanding population. We don't as yet have a border dispute with Dhaba, but everyone knows it will happen someday. Can we afford to let Dhaba have a weapon we can't match? Particularly one as devastating as this."

"All right," Grofield said. "I see the way it runs."

"We would all rather spend the money elsewhere," she said. "Some of us on schools, others on yachts. No one wants to bring home a sealed metal jar full of death, costing more than one citizen's average annual income for a thousand years, knowing we will only put it on a shelf and never use it. But we have to, we have no choice. As long as it's available, we have to get our share."

"Goody," Grofield said. "But why the whole weekend? And why all those hotel reservations down in Quebec, if the main event is up here?"

"We were to gather in Quebec," she said, "and then be brought up here. The people selling don't trust anyone any more than they have to, so no one knew exactly where the meeting would take place until we were all brought up here. And the deal was to have been completed tomorrow morning. Most of us would have been back in Quebec by tomorrow night, and there was going to be a conference the next day, on Sunday. The different leaders had a lot of things to discuss, spheres of influence, temporary partnerships against other nations, our relationships with the major powers, things like that. That would have been done on Sunday. Then on Monday everyone would go home. A few people would have stayed up here until then, including you."

"Why?"

"We couldn't let you go until everything was finished and we were all on our way home."

"Why were the other people going to stay here?"

"It was agreed the sellers would stay here until Monday. We didn't want them betraying us, announcing to the American or Canadian authorities about what we were carrying with us."

"Everybody trusts everybody," Grofield said.

"All the trusters are dead," she said.

"I believe you. All right, let me think for a minute."

"Go right ahead," she said.

He went right ahead, but without pleasure. All his thoughts were depressing.

Given what Vivian had told him, he could fill in most of the rest for himself. These bucket-shop plutocrats, Rahgos and Pozos and the other colonels and generals, not used to secrecy at the big time level, had left tracks in the sand and some of the bigger predators had come wandering by. The Americans had found out that something was going on, but not what, and had shipped Grofield in here real quick to get the details. And somebody else —Russia, maybe, or China, or maybe France, Egypt, Israel, Argentina, you name it—had also become aware of all the activity, and had tried more direct means of gaining its information, such as kidnapping Grofield and planning to inject him with truth serum.

He said, "Are you missing anybody from your party? Anybody lost, strayed, or stolen?"

"Not that I know of," she said. "Before tonight, you mean."

"Before coming up here."

"No."

"Somebody did, I bet," he said. "They got to somebody from one of the national groups, the way they tried to get to me, and they found out what was going on, and they came up here to get the goodies for themselves."

"But who are they?"

"I don't know. They speak a language I don't recognize. One of them was with a Free Quebec organization, but this deal is on a higher order of insanity than that."

"They're the ones who killed your friend?"

"Hardly my friend. But they're the ones, you're right. They sure do believe in direct action. But I don't know how they expect to get away with this stunt. Are they just going to bump off the presidents of nine different countries?"

"Why not?" she said. "There are men in every one of those capital cities just hoping and praying their leader doesn't return from this trip. By Tuesday there will be nine bloodless revolutions, nine deposed presidents, whereabouts unknown, and most of it won't even get into the world's newspapers."

"Better and better," Grofield said.

"It's up to us to get those canisters," she said.

He tried to look at her, even though he couldn't see a thing. "Are you out of your mind? That lodge is crawling with armed men. Do *you* know where the canisters are?"

"No. No one knows but the four Americans."

"Fine. So we'd have to go over to the lodge and round up one of the Americans and get him to tell us where the canisters are.

Then we'd have to go get them and take them away. All without being seen or stopped by the guys from the airplane. Frankly, Vivian, I have my doubts."

Urgently she said, "But we don't know who they are! We don't know what they plan to do with the canisters. Maybe fly over New York City and Washington and London and Paris and drop them. None of us would have done anything like that, none of us would have had the reason or the desire to do it, or enough to do it even if we wanted to. We would have kept it as a defense, a warning, a kind of ultimatum. The same way the Americans keep it. But we don't know who these other people are or what they want to do. And they seem to choose killing more often than not."

"I'd rather not give them the chance," Grofield said, "of choosing to kill me. If you don't mind. I have no objection to playing the fool in order to save the world, but not if I don't have the slightest chance of surviving or of doing anybody any good."

"But we have to *try*! What else are you going to do?"

"I've been thinking about that," he said, "and it seems to me the only sensible thing for me to do is get on my trusty skimobile and head south at first light. What that plane can do in one hour I should be able to do in four or five in my skimobile, and maybe even before then I'll come to a settlement or something with a telephone. Or a radio, I'm not picky. Then I'll call good old Ken in Quebec and tell him the story and tell him to send the Marines up to the snowy North Woods and put the arm on the baddies."

"They'll be gone long before that," she said angrily, "and you know it. That isn't any good, you know it isn't any good."

"I know," Grofield agreed gloomily. "It isn't any good. But boy, it's what I want to do."

"We have to think of something else."

He sighed. "All right. How many people know where these canisters are?"

"Just the four Americans," she said.

"And they're somewhere around the lodge? Inside one of the buildings?"

"I don't think so. The impression I got was that they were hidden somewhere not very far away, but not exactly *at* the lodge."

"All right. Do you know what these four Americans look like?"

"Yes."

"All four of them? You could point them out to me?"

"Yes, of course."

"Okay." He got reluctantly to his feet. "Let's have some light," he said. "We have to reorganize our supplies."

The flashlight clicked on, and in its pale light he saw her frowning at him in cautious hope. "You have an idea?"

"We can call it an idea," he said, folding his blanket.

"What is it?"

"I'm not telling you."

She was astonished. "Why not?"

"Because I'm not sure you'd approve," he said.

TWENTY-FOUR

"THIS IS CLOSE ENOUGH," Grofield said, and stopped the skimobile.

Sitting behind him, arms wrapped around him again, the girl said, "What do we do now?"

"Walk the rest of the way," he said.

They had repacked the skimobile, leaving more room for Vivian in back, and then Grofield had driven back out onto the lake and traveled about halfway across toward the lodge before making a sharp left and heading toward the shore. They'd had to make brief intermittent use of the flashlight, there being no longer any star-shine at all to guide themselves by. The last few stars were winking out far above the lodge, apparently being covered by a cloud mass moving down from the north. The breeze had sharpened a bit, but was not yet a real wind. Grofield's cheeks were numb, though, and his fingers were aching again despite the thicker gloves. He wasn't sure if that meant it was getting colder out or if it was just the result of his continued exposure.

In any case, with sparing use of the flashlight they'd guided themselves to shore and had then traveled over the dunes in a great half circle around the lodge, until the buildings were between them and the lake. And now Grofield had stopped, a good distance from the buildings, but close enough to see their lights. From this side, the red smudge of embers could be seen where the burned-out dormitory had once stood.

Grofield and Vivian got up from the skimobile and Grofield said, "We won't take anything but the guns and the flashlight. We'll need that to follow our tracks back here again."

"If we live," she said.

"I intend to live," he told her. "After all the things I've been involved in in my life, to be killed up here in the back of nowhere in the middle of somebody else's stupid squabble would be too ridiculous to contemplate. I'm not going to get killed because I refuse to be made a fool of. Come on."

It was slow work, walking through the soft snow, but warming. When Grofield heard Vivian panting beside him, he slowed his pace a little. Two minutes one way or the other wouldn't make that much difference.

The slower pace helped her, and she got her breath back enough to say, "Shouldn't you tell me your plan now? How will I know what to do when we get there?"

"Your job is to point," Grofield told her. "We are going to snoop around over there until we find your four Americans."

"Do you think they'll tell you where the canisters are because you're another American? How will you be able to talk to them without being caught?"

"All in good time," Grofield said. "Don't talk, it wastes breath."

"But I want to know," she said.

"Besides," he said, "we're getting too close. They might have outside guards."

"In weather like this?"

"Hush."

She hushed, and they moved in silence toward the buildings. Directly ahead was the lodge, with the remaining dormitory on an angle back to its left. That was the building Grofield had been briefly imprisoned in. Symmetrically to the right of the lodge was the smoldering remnant of the other dormitory, and beyond that the storage building from which Grofield had stolen the skimobile. The three remaining buildings all contained lit windows, so all would be occupied by the invaders, whoever they were.

There were no outside floodlights, an unexpected blessing in a place like this. Or maybe not so unexpected, given the climate. There would rarely be anything outside to look at except snow.

Still, light-spill from the windows did give some illumination to the snow outside, so the closer they got to the buildings the slower Grofield moved. He was beginning to wish he was dressed like Finnish ski troops, in white uniform and white skis. Of course, Vivian dressed like that could be a little startling, nothing showing except the black face, the Cheshire Cat as done by Eartha Kitt

She said, "What are you chuckling about?"

"A mental image," he said.

"You're weird," she said.

"You must be right," Grofield said, "or I wouldn't be here at all. Now hush."

"Mm." One syllable, but full of muted mutiny.

Grofield was moving now at an oblique angle, toward the dormitory building on the left. Of the fifteen or so windows along the side, no more than five were lit. But if a guard were on duty to watch the outside, he wouldn't be in a lit room, he'd sit in darkness, so he would be able to see out without the window mirroring the room behind him. It was the dark windows he had to be wary of, not the lit ones.

He stopped a dozen yards from the building and crouched in the snow, pulling Vivian down beside him. He whispered, "We're going into that building there. It's a long hall inside, with rooms on both sides. Like a hotel. There's an exit door at each end, and we're going to the nearest one. We're going to go around in a curve and try to keep away from any light shining out. You'll follow me, and if I stop, you stop. If I drop to the ground, you drop. And be silent."

"All right."

"And if I turn around and start running, you do the same."

"Don't worry. What if you start shooting?"

"Guess," he whispered. "Come on."

They moved forward again, Grofield in the lead, and came around slowly to the end of the dormitory building. There were no windows on either end, just the doors, with small panes of glass showing the lit hallway inside. They reached the door without being seen and Grofield looked through the glass. The hall was empty. He tried the door and it was unlocked, and he and Vivian slipped quickly inside.

"Flashlight," he whispered.

She removed a glove, took the flashlight from her pocket, put the glove in the pocket.

He nodded at the first door on the right. "Stand to the side of that door," he whispered. "When I open it, stick your arm over and shine the light in. But don't get in the doorway."

"All right."

She got in position, and nodded that she was ready. He held the machine gun in his right hand and reached forward to the doorknob with his left. He shoved the door open and the light shone in and the room was empty.

"Okay," he whispered. "Now the other side."

The same thing on the other side, the flashlight shone on an empty room.

They worked their way down the hall that way. About half the room doors were open, and they could be more quickly checked. Three were locked from the outside and Grofield kicked the doors in. And when they were done they had found no one, the building was except for themselves completely empty.

Grofield stood frowning in the corridor when they were done checking the place out. "They must have a smaller force than I thought," he said. "All concentrated in the main building."

"So what do we do now?"

"We go over there. But we be careful about it."

"Good."

He went down to the door at the end of the corridor, and looked through the glass at the main building. Most of the windows were lit, giving the place a festive air. Yuletide cheer, all that. He stood at the window, watching, and after about a minute he saw a dark shape moving along outside the wall, silhouetted when passing in front of a window, invisible until the next window. He was moving from right to left along the rear of the building, and when he got to the corner, invisible for just a second, he turned around and went back the other way. Meaning there was probably another man walking a post along the side of the building. Grofield squinted in that direction and after a minute saw him. Another dark shape, hunch-shouldered, bulky, moving gloomily along outside the warm windows.

Behind him Vivian said, "Do you see anything?"

"Guards," Grofield said, and turned to look at her. "They have four outside guards, one on each side of the building. Moving, not stationary."

"What are we going to do?"

Grofield turned and looked out the window again. He couldn't see either of the guards at first, but then he picked them both up. "They aren't happy," he said. "Unhappy guards are not alert guards. Come here and watch. Can you see them?"

She came, the two of them pressed together at the small window, the fur of her hat brushing the side of his face. "No," she said.

"Look along the back wall," he said. "Third lit window from the left. He's going to pass that in just a second, from left to right. Now!"

"Yes! I see him. If you hadn't told me, I'd never have found him at all."

"All right," Grofield said. "I'm going over there. You keep watching that third window. When the coast is clear I'll stand so that window's behind me and I'll wave my arm over my head. I'll only do it once, so keep your eyes open."

"I will."

"And bring my gun when you come."

"You aren't taking it with you?"

"I won't want noise over there," he said.

"But just in case—"

"It'll slow me down," he said. "You keep watching there. This shouldn't take longer than ten minutes."

"All right," she said.

Grofield walked back down the corridor, stopping off in one of the lit rooms where he'd noticed a lamp on a bedside table. He unplugged the lamp, put it on the floor, stood on it, wrapped the wire around his gloved hand, and yanked the wire loose from the lamp. He wrapped the rest of the wire around his hand, tucked in the end, and left the room.

He continued down the corridor and went out the rear door, the same way he and Vivian had come in. He turned right and walked away from the building far enough so none of the lit windows would betray him, then walked down the length of it to the other end and then back toward the building again until he stood against the corner of it. The lodge was dead ahead, and the door behind which Vivian was waiting was just to his right.

He squinted until he picked up both of the guards, and watched their movements for a while. They had different length beats to walk, the one on the side having much less territory to cover, so they rarely met at the corner, which was good. Grofield waited till one time when they did meet, and then both were going away, their backs to him, and at that point he ran forward, heading for the corner of the lodge, coming in at the angle at which he was least likely to be seen from any window. He moved as fast as he could through the snow, was breathing hard when he reached the lodge wall, and leaned there for a second till he'd caught his breath. Then he moved to the right.

The space between the second and third windows was the

widest darkness along the rear wall, a fact he'd noted while watching from inside the dormitory. Grofield went halfway between those two windows and dropped to his knees against the wall. He ducked his head down and crouched into a ball, making himself as small as possible. There he busily unwrapped most of the wire from around his hand, left some, wrapped the other end around his other hand.

He was now in darkness, against a dark wall, a small indistinct lump. The guard would pass by soon, gloomy, thinking about other things, wishing his tour of outside duty was up, and it was unlikely he would even see this low bump of darkness against the wall of the building, much less pay any attention to what he was seeing.

Grofield waited, listening, and it seemed a long time before he heard the plodding thud of the guard's footsteps coming this way, following the trough he had worn in the snow, out half a dozen feet from the edge of the building, a path he'd apparently chosen because it gave him a chance to walk in the light of the windows.

Grofield listened, not moving, waiting for the first sign of hesitancy in the footsteps, but they came steadily, unenthusiastically on. They slogged on by Grofield, and the instant they were past him Grofield raised his head, looked over his shoulder, and saw the bowed head of the guard, who was walking along with a Bren gun in his hands.

Grofield got to his feet. He could do that silently, but he couldn't move silently through snow, so the next part had to be fast, and it had to be done before the guard reached the next window's illumination. Grofield ran forward, his arms up over his head, and as the startled guard was turning around Grofield was on him, bringing his arms down, reversing them, the wire flipping over the guard's head.

The guard was trying to turn around, trying to aim the Bren gun, trying to keep Grofield from getting behind him, but it was too late. Grofield closed his right hand on the guard's left shoulder from behind, yanked him around, shoved his knee into the small of the guard's back, and spread his arms as wide as they would go, which closed the loop of wire around the guard's throat.

The guard thrashed, gurgling, trying to call out. The Bren gun dropped into the snow, his gloved hands clawed at the wire. He struggled hard enough to knock them both over, and they landed on their sides, but it only relaxed Grofield's tension on the wire for a second, and then he had it as strong as ever. The guard kept struggling, kicking snow in the air, waving his hands behind his head in a wild attempt to get at Grofield, and Grofield gritted his teeth and held the wire taut.

Slowly the guard's struggles weakened, but soon it was possible for Grofield to get up onto his knees, force the guard's body face-down, then kneel on his back and finish the job.

He left the wire where it was, and got to his feet. He was panting, and at first he just stood there and waited for the nerves jumping in his arms and shoulders to calm down. Then he walked over to the trapezoid of illumination from the third window, raised an arm over his head, and waved it.

TWENTY-FIVE

"HERE," SHE WHISPERED, and handed Grofield his machine gun.

"Thanks."

"Where is he?"

Grofield motioned the machine gun at the shape lying half covered by snow. She looked at it, then frowned at Grofield. "You killed him?"

"Naturally. Come on."

She hesitated a second or two, then followed him, and the two of them trudged through the soft snow against the building wall. The guard's path was inviting out there, five or six feet from the wall, but it went directly through all the illumination. In here they were in shadow, and they could stoop under the windows, whose sills were a good five feet off the ground.

Grofield led the way to the rear door he remembered from yesterday afternoon. It was unlocked, and the hall inside was empty. He opened the door and stepped in, she came in quickly after him, and he shut the door again.

There were half a dozen side doors down the length of the hall, three on each side, but Grofield ignored them. The four Americans were unlikely to be anywhere without a guard on the door. If he didn't find them elsewhere in here, he'd come back. Right now, though, he went directly to the far end of the hall and the door that led to the library. It was closed, and when he put his ear against it he heard murmurs of conversation from inside. He stepped away, leaned close to Vivian, whispered, "We're going in there. Show them the gun, but don't use it unless you absolutely have to."

She nodded. She looked a little shaky, strained and tense around the eyes, but her mouth was determined.

He asked, "You going to be all right?"

She nodded, not saying anything.

He patted her shoulder, and reached out to the doorknob. He shoved the door open and stepped quickly in and to the left, so the people inside would see Vivian right away and know there were two guns to contend with.

There were four men in the room, broad-faced Caucasians with heavy shoulders and brown or black hair. They'd been sitting around a table playing some sort of card game, but now they dropped their cards and pushed their chairs back from the table with squealing noises of chair legs on the wooden floor. Their faces looked startled, but not frightened.

"Not a sound," Grofield said, and gestured with the machine gun because he wasn't sure they would understand English.

They understood the gun. There was a long tense instant when nothing happened, nobody moved, nothing had been decided one way or the other, and then one of them slowly lifted his hands up over his head. The others glanced at him, and did the same thing.

Not taking his eyes off them, Grofield said, "Vivian, put your gun down where none of them can reach it. Circle around behind them, without getting between me and them. Then get their guns."

"Yes," she said. He didn't dare look over at her, but her voice sounded strong and capable.

He kept watching the four cardplayers, seeing Vivian in motion out of the corner of his eye. She did it right, circling around behind them, frisking them without giving any of them a chance to get hold of her and use her for a shield. Two of them had pistols inside their coats, the other two were clean.

Vivian looked around, then pointed at a far corner. "They have guns over there."

"All right." Grofield gestured at them with the gun again. "Lie down," he said.

They looked blank.

Grofield held the gun in one hand and pointed at the floor with the other. "Down," he said. He made a spread-out-flat gesture, palm down.

The one who'd been the first to raise his hands now was the first to move again. A questioning look on his face, *is this right?* he lowered himself to one knee, his hands still raised over his head.

Grofield nodded.

Tentatively, the other lowered his hands, then lay down on his stomach. The others hesitated, but Grofield made angry gestures with the gun and they followed suit. Then Grofield said, "Vivian, use their shoelaces to tie their wrists and ankles. Rip up their shirttails for gags."

"Woman's work is never done," she said, and got to it, with Grofield standing on. She did the tying first, and then Grofield could put the gun down and help her with the gagging.

The guns leaning against the wall in the far corner were Brens, like the one the guard outside had carried. Originally a British light machine gun with an open metal stock, the design had been copied everywhere, and Bren guns now came from Yugoslavia, from Israel, from all over the world. So that wouldn't tell anything about where these people came from.

Grofield went over to where they were lying on the floor, frisked one of them, and found a passport. The name of the coun-

try would be on the front, of course, and so it was: SHQIP-
ENIJA.

Oh for Christ's sake. Grofield leafed through the passport, saw
that passport photos were just as badly done in Shqipenija as in
the United States, and learned that the owner of the passport was
named Gjul Enver Shkumbi and he'd been born in Shkodër,
Shqipenija, on the twenty-second of some incomprehensible
month in 1928.

Vivian came over, saying, "What are you doing?"

"Trying to figure out where these people come from," he said,
and handed her the passport. "That make any sense to you?"

She glanced at it. "Albania," she said, and handed it back.

"Albania?" He frowned at the passport again. "If it's Albania,
why doesn't it say Albania?"

She said, "Because they don't speak English in Albania, they
speak Shqyp." She pronounced it *shkyip*. "And in Shqyp," she
went on, "Albania is Shqipenija. That means eagle country."

"Oh does it." Grofield shook his head, and dropped the passport on its owner. "Albania," he said. "That means they're working for Russia, huh?"

"Probably not," she said.

Grofield frowned at her. "Aren't they Communists?"

"I keep forgetting how nonpolitical you are," she said. "Albania tends to be more in the Chinese camp than the Russian.
The Chinese often use Albanian agents in parts of the world
where Chinese agents would be too obvious."

"These people are working for *China?*"

"Probably. But Albania is a Warsaw Treaty member, so it is
possible they're working for the Russians, but the Russians prefer
to use their own people. They could even be working for Yugoslavia, though I doubt it."

"Oh, shut up," Grofield said. "You know, my buddy Ken told
me some of the Free Quebec outfits were Maoist, with Communist Chinese connections. Would that make sense? The Chinese

found out there was something going on, sent in their Albanian friends and had them link up with one of the wilder Free Quebec groups for local assistance. How does that sound?"

"It sounds right," she said. "And I think we definitely don't want the Chinese to get those canisters. They're not afraid of anything, those people, they'd shoot off a toe to get rid of a corn."

"That's graphic," Grofield said. "All right, let's get on with it." He went over to the opposite door and slowly turned the knob. The door opened inward, and he cracked it just an inch, peering through the slit at the main room.

It didn't look much changed. Some of the furniture was knocked over, and a couple of windows were broken, but they were the only signs of the battle that had raged here earlier tonight. As it had been when Grofield had first come here, the middle area of the room was empty, the occupants clustered around the fireplaces at both ends. With the broken windows, they had even more reason for that now. And the result, from Grofield's point of view, was a positive good, since it meant there was no one at all near this door.

He opened the door a little wider, and studied the people down at the far end of the room. He recognized Marba down there, but no one else, and it was clear who were the prisoners and who were the guards. The prisoners, seven or eight of them, sat in a morose huddle near the fire, with the three guards on chairs a little farther away, guns resting on their laps. There didn't seem to be any conversation going on down there at all.

Grofield moved back from the door and motioned Vivian over, whispering, "Look down to the left. Any of our four down there?"

She stood against the wall and peered through the opening, taking her time, but finally stepping back and shaking her head.

Grofield gently pushed the door closed again and said, "It's going to be trickier looking the other way. You wouldn't have a mirror on you, would you?"

"Of course I have. A girl doesn't travel without her compact."

"She doesn't?"

She took a round compact from her jacket pocket, and held it up. "She doesn't."

"Good. What you do, when I open the door again you hold that out just far enough so you can see the people at the other end. Try to make it as fast as you can, and try not to move the mirror around very much. We don't want anybody's eye attracted by glints and reflections."

She nodded. "I'll do it fast," she promised.

They got into position, and Grofield opened the door again, just enough for her to extend the open compact through. She closed one eye and squinted the other, studying the reflection in the mirror, turning it slightly twice, then bringing it back in again. Grofield shut the door, and Vivian shook her head, saying, "Not there either."

"They have to make it tough," Grofield commented. "They've probably got them locked away upstairs someplace for safekeeping. I wish I knew how much these people knew."

"From the way they act," she said, "they know everything except where the canisters are."

"So they'd know to keep the four Americans separate and under heavy guard. All right, let's go see how many ways there are to get upstairs."

They crossed the room to the door they'd come in, and Grofield was just reaching for the knob when Vivian grabbed his arm and whispered, "Listen!"

He listened, and heard the sounds of boots on stairs. Ba-thump, ba-thump, and the sounds of people talking. A group coming down a flight of stairs, then coming right by this door and going on down the hall toward the rear exit.

"Damn!" Grofield muttered.

She said, "What is it?"

"Relief," Grofield told her. "They're on their way outside to take over guard duty."

"That's bad," she said.

"I couldn't agree more." He stood leaning his head against the door, listening, and as soon as he heard the outer door open he yanked the knob and hurried out to the hall, moving so fast he saw the last of the relief guards going out down at the farther end of the hall.

The hall was L-shaped, the bottom leg going off briefly to the right, ending at a flight of stairs leading upward. Grofield said, "From now on we have to move very fast and not worry about noise. Come on."

They raced up the stairs, Grofield taking them three at a time, up nine steps to a landing, then reverse and up six more to the second floor, entering on the top left of a T-shaped hall. There was no one in sight along the top bar, but when he reached the middle and looked down the long hallway to his right he saw three men with Bren guns sitting on chairs in front of a closed door midway down on the left. He braced his feet and fired a burst from the machine gun, spraying them, and they flipped over all at once, like a sand castle demolished by an invisible tide.

Grofield ran forward, and out of a room on the right came two startled men, guns in their hands. Grofield fired hastily at them, and one fell but the other ducked back out of sight. Grofield ran past that doorway, seeing a dozen more of them in there, and shouted back to Vivian, just rounding the turn back there, "Keep them bottled up!" He pointed the machine gun at the doorway he meant. "Stay there and keep them bottled up!"

"I will!"

He ran on to the doorway guarded by the three dead men and tried the knob. It was locked. He kicked the door, and it held firm.

Someone inside shouted, "Watch it, there's two in here!"

Vivian's gun chattered, and Grofield looked down the hall in time to see somebody ducking back into the squad room. He shouted, "Vivian, for Christ's sake, no warning shots! If you get a chance at them, kill them!"

"I've never done it!"

"You'll never get a better chance!" Grofield shouted, and the squad-room door slammed shut. An unexpected blessing. Grofield gestured wildly at Vivian to come to him, and held his finger to his lips. She nodded, and hurried silently down the hall, and Grofield told her, "Stand beside the door, and shoot when you see something to shoot at."

"All right." She was on the edge of hysteria, but was keeping it fiercely under control.

Grofield stood to the other side of the door and fired a burst at the lock. He could hear commotion downstairs now, knew they'd be coming up soon. Keeping clear of the doorway, he kicked the door open.

Gunfire chattered inside, and plaster flew from the opposite wall. The same voice that had shouted the warning before now yelled, "They're behind the sofa!"

Grofield said, "Vivian. Fire into the room. Don't show yourself, just stick the barrel around the door and start shooting."

She nodded shakily and did so. Grofield counted to three, and dove through the doorway under the line of her fire. He hit the floor rolling, kept rolling until he hit a piece of furniture, found it to be an overstuffed chair, and clambered quickly behind it, feeling it shiver as bullets thudded into it.

Vivian screamed, and yelled, "They're coming up!"

"Hold them!" Grofield yelled, and stuck his gun around the other side of the sofa and pulled the trigger. He followed the gun around, saw the overturned sofa in the middle of the room, broadside to the door, saw that the angle he'd gotten to made the sofa poor protection for the two white men behind it, saw the four black men lying self-protectively on the floor against the far wall, and kept firing. One of the white men screamed and fell back, and the other one ran for a safer piece of furniture. Grofield cut him down in mid-stride and yelled, "Vivian, come in!"

She backed in, looking terrified and hysterical. "They're all over out there!"

Grofield shouted, "Is this them?" and pointed at the four black men getting to their feet.

She looked in panicky distraction at them and said, "Yes, yes."

"All four?"

"Yes! That's them, Grofield, for God's sake that's them!"

One of the four said to Grofield, "I don't know where you came from, man, but you're beautiful." All four of them were grinning in relief.

Grofield said, "Did you tell anybody where the canisters are?"

"Are you crazy? That's what's kept us alive."

"Nobody at all?" Grofield insisted.

"Not even the chaplain," the spokesman said.

"That's good," Grofield said, and pointed the machine gun at them, and pulled the trigger.

TWENTY-SIX

Vivian screamed and jumped forward to knock the gun barrel down, but she was too late. She stared in disbelief from the falling bodies to Grofield, shrieking, "Why? What did you do it for?"

"Now nobody knows where the canisters are," Grofield told her. "Come on, let's get out of here." He hurried to the window, unlocked it, pushed it open.

"You *murdered* them."

"Do you know how to do a cannonball dive?"

"You murdered them!"

Grofield angrily grabbed her arm and shook her. "Bitch at me later! I'm not going to get killed to give you a chance to nag. Do you know how to do a cannonball dive? You wrap your arms around your legs, bend your knees up—"

"I know how," she said. She looked and sounded dazed.

"Then do one out the window," he told her. "Don't worry, the snow's soft. Then head for the building we were in before."

"I can't believe . . . " She was looking at the bodies again.

"God *damn* it!" Grofield yelled, and picked her up, and threw her out the window. She'd dropped her machine gun when he grabbed her, and he threw that out after her, then threw his own machine gun and jumped.

The snow wasn't as soft as he'd remembered. It was a tooth-rattling landing, and he got up dazed, barely remembering the fact of urgency, losing for a second or two the circumstances. He knew he was supposed to run, though, and started off through the snow, but then got enough of his brains together to remember the guns. He stopped and looked back, and they were nowhere in sight, they'd sunk into the snow without a trace. He took a step back, and somebody started shooting at him from the window he'd just left, so he turned around and ran the other way again, seeing a vague splash of green bobbing ahead of him. Vivian's ski pants.

After floundering toward the other building for a while, he stumbled across the path between it and the lodge, and then he could go faster. He caught up with Vivian just as she reached the building, and took her arm. "We'll go through it," he said. "It'll be faster."

She pulled away from him. "I'll take my chances on my own," she said.

"We don't have time for stupidity, Vivian," he said, and opened the door and shoved her inside. There was still the odd chatter of gunfire from behind them, but it had to be people shooting at shadows, and when Grofield looked back he couldn't see anyone yet actually outside the building and pursuing them. It would happen, but that crowd over there would need a couple of minutes to get itself organized.

Grofield went into the building, and she was standing just inside, glaring at him. He said, "I killed them because it was the only way to handle it."

"You killed them," she said, "because they were black."

He stared at her. "Are you out of your mind?"

"Americans have a reputation," she said. "I see it's well-earned."

"Vivian," he said, "I couldn't carry those four with me. I couldn't guard them. I had to shut their mouths before anybody injected them with truth serum."

"You wouldn't have killed them if they were white," she said.

"The hell I wouldn't. Don't you realize they would have had to kill *me?*"

She frowned at him. "Don't be stupid," she said. "You were saving their lives, why should they kill you?"

"Because I'm an American, working at the moment for the government, and I know too damn much about those four. I could blow the whistle on them when we all got back to the States, and nothing would convince them I'd keep my mouth shut. I could have done it the other way, I could have had all six of us jump out the window, and then we'd all run over to here, and at some point one of the four would manage to get behind me, and that would be the end of it. Given the fact that they were up here to peddle instant death for the whole world to anybody with the price, I really doubt they were Boy Scouts."

"Neither are you," she said. "It isn't as though you're a policeman."

"You know the background on me," Grofield reminded her. "They didn't. All they'd know is I'm the American spy that was brought up here to be put on ice for the weekend. I'd smell like cop to them, I'd smell like all kinds of trouble to them. I did the only thing I could do, I saw to it that *nobody* would get those canisters, and I protected myself." He looked through the glass in the door and said, "We'd better argue this out later. Here come the people from eagle country."

She went willingly with him now, and he led the way down the long hall and out the door at the far end. She got out the flashlight and they followed their own footsteps back toward the skimobile. The trail was faint already, the breeze smoothing it out. Also, the first snowflakes of a new fall were already starting down.

The pursuit was quite a ways behind them, but well-equipped

with lights. Looking back, Grofield could see the glare of large lanterns back there and knew the pursuers would be having no trouble following their trail through the snow. As long as they were all on foot, though, it didn't much matter.

The skimobile was where they'd left it, lightly powdered with new snow. They got aboard and Grofield switched on the engine and headlight and drove them away from there.

They traveled in silence for ten minutes, curving in a great loop around to the right, the lights of the lodge frequently out of sight, and the snowfall gradually increasing in intensity. By the time they came around to the lake again it was a heavy slanting fall, being driven by an ever-strengthening wind. They weren't all the way across the lake from the lodge this time, Grofield having stopped about halfway around the shore.

He turned around when he got to the edge of the lake and put a snow dune between himself and the lights of the lodge before stopping. Then he and Vivian got off and stretched and she said, "What now?"

"We bed down here," he said.

"Till when?"

"Till morning."

"Then what?"

"I don't know. Depends. If the storm is over, I'd like to try driving south and see where we come out. If the plane comes back for our shpikee-tikee friends—"

"Shqipenija," she said.

"That's what I said. If the plane comes back and takes them away, we can go over there and see if they have a radio. It depends what the circumstances are." He turned to untie the blankets from the skimobile.

She touched his arm. "Grofield."

He looked around.

"You may have been right about those four guys," she said. "Anyway, I believe you about why you did it."

"I should think so," he said, and handed her her blanket.

$\mathcal{S}$

TWENTY-SEVEN

$\mathcal{S}$

"GROFIELD!"

He was freezing, and somebody was jostling his shoulder. His face was covered by a cold damp blanket, and when he pushed it away snow spattered all over his face and neck.

He sat up, shocked awake by the cold, to find he'd been covered by nearly an inch of powdery snow overnight. It was daylight now and no longer snowing, though the sky was covered completely with gray clouds, as though the earth was wearing a shower cap.

"I missed sunrise!" he said, starting to get up, but she tugged him violently down again and he fell amid another little swirl of snow. "What the hell?"

"The plane's back!" She was talking in a hushed whisper, as though the plane were hulking just past her shoulder.

It wasn't. Grofield looked at her, blinking, and said, "When did it get here?"

"I don't know. I just woke up a minute ago, and there it was."

Grofield got to his feet, and went up the snow dune at a sham-

179

bling crouch until he could see over the top, and there was the plane. He could see now it wasn't the same one that had brought him up here, but it was the same or a similar model. He watched for a minute, and nothing happened around the plane, and he went back down to where Vivian was waiting. "I suppose the thing to do," he said, "is wait and see what happens next."

"Do you think they'll leave?"

"Nobody there knows where the canisters are. The snow wiped out our trail, so even if they think I know where they are they can't come after me to ask. I can't think of any reason for them to stay."

"I hope you're right," she said. "God, how I want to get warm again."

"While we're waiting, let's eat."

"I wish we could have a fire."

"Keep on wishing," he said unhelpfully.

They ate cold canned food, sitting on their folded blankets, and were just finishing when they heard the plane engines, a faint sound, muffled by all the fresh soft snow. They climbed to the top of the dune again and watched the troops loading into the plane across the way. It didn't take long, and then the plane cumbersomely turned around and rolled slowly past from right to left. At the far end of the lake it turned again and came back, this time steadily gaining speed and finally lifting into the air, raising its nose toward the clouds.

Grofield watched it climb until it was way up, then looked across the lake at the lodge. "We'll give them a chance to get out of sight," he said, "and then we'll—"

"Look!"

He looked at her, and she was staring skyward. He followed her gaze, and there were three planes in the sky all at once, the lumbering cargo plane and two slender, darting sharks. "Where the hell did they come from?"

"They dropped out of the clouds," she said. "They're Migs." She looked at him. "Russian."

"Who's minding the UN? Everybody's here."

They watched the three planes, saw the two Migs zooming past the heavier plane, flashing by and then turning to make another pass. They couldn't hear the firing, but they saw the black smoke start on the cargo plane's right engine, saw the plane seem to dip as though tired, saw it falter, and then all at once it was falling out of the sky, the Migs circling higher, fading into the clouds before the plane hit the ground far away. A pillar of smoke rose up black to mark the place where it had hit.

"It looks to me," Grofield said quietly, "as though *nobody* wanted the Chinese to get that stuff."

$$

TWENTY-EIGHT

$$

GROFIELD STOOD AT THE WINDOW of his room in the Chateau Frontenac, frowning at the walls outside. "The United States Government is very cheap, Ken," he said. "They wouldn't even spring for a room with a view."

Ken said, "Never mind the view. Let's finish your statement."

Grofield turned away from the window. "It is finished," he said. "The cargo plane took off, the Russian planes shot it down, Vivian and I went over to the lodge and found that everybody still alive had been locked up in rooms on the second floor. We let them out and they radioed their pilot down in Roberval and we all came home. Three of the government heads had been killed in the fighting, Colonel Rahgos of Undurwa and two others. I'm sorry, I didn't get their names or countries."

"We'll find out eventually. Are you sure these were Russian planes? Did you see any markings?"

"Vivian told me they were Migs, that's all I know. They didn't get low enough to see markings."

Ken nodded, and glanced at his notes. "You're lucky that bunch decided to bring you back and not leave you up there with a bullet in your head."

"Vivian was on my side," Grofield said. "And we didn't tell them I was the one who killed the four Americans. The whole operation was a bust anyway, so they didn't have anything to gain by killing me." Grofield stretched hugely and hugely yawned. "You may not believe this, buddy of my life," he said, "but I am tired. Why don't you go away now, and if you have any more questions write them out on a slip of paper and shove them under the door? Or somewhere."

"This should do it," Ken said, and got to his feet. "I must admit I'd thought you'd run out on us, Grofield."

"I must admit I would have liked to," Grofield said.

"Well, you came through. You're a free agent from now on, we're pulling out. You have this room paid for till Monday anyway, if you want it."

"I'll probably sleep till then."

"Do that. I expect we'll have to wait till spring to go up there and look for those canisters. We'll find them, though."

"Wonderful," Grofield said, and yawned again.

"Well, I'll let you get some sleep." Ken stuck his hand out. "We do appreciate it," he said.

Grofield looked at the hand in astonishment, but then took it, mostly because if he did Ken's ritual with him maybe then Ken would leave. "If you ever need me again," he said, "I want you to know you'll have to blackmail me."

Ken chuckled, and left.

Grofield went into the bathroom and turned on the shower, and while the water was getting hot he stripped out of his clothes. He hadn't had them off since first putting them on in the back of that truck a day and a half ago, and in the intervening time he'd done a lot of strenuous moving around.

A nice shower, and then sleep. He stepped into the tub and let the hot water roll over his body. The frozen north was just a dream, just a dream.

He walked back into the bedroom drying himself, and there was Vivian, sitting in the same chair. Grofield stood flat-footed, looking at her. "Oh, come on," he said. "I'm tired."

She was smiling. "Colonel Marba sent me down," she said, "to express his appreciation for everything you've done for him."

"*Colonel* Marba?"

"No one at home knows about Colonel Rahgos's death yet," she said, and the smile widened. "They'll learn about it from his successor."

"My best to Colonel Marba," Grofield said, and went over to the bed and lay down and pulled the covers over himself.

She got up from the chair and came over to the bed and sat down beside him. "And I wanted to thank you, too," she said. "For everything you've done for me."

"Is that right."

"And to tell you your room isn't bugged any more. All the microphones are gone."

He looked at her with renewed interest. "Is that right?"

Quite a while later, she said, "Remember the snotty thing I said to you the very first time I saw you?"

"Sure."

"Well, I was wrong."

"Oh, that," Grofield said. "That's a common misconception. It has to do with a physiological difference between the races when flaccid."

"So I see," she said.

"But there's no difference while operational," Grofield explained.

"I love scientific men," she said.